His
REBOUND
Bitch

KIKI SWINSON
NEW YORK TIMES BEST SELLING AUTHOR

This is a work of fiction. All of the characters, organizations, and events portrayed in this novel are either products of the author's imagination or are used fictitiously.

Publisher's address:
K.S. Publications
P.O. Box 68878
Virginia Beach, VA 23471

Website: www.kikiswinson.net
Email: KS.publications@yahoo.com

ISBN-13: 978-0985349592
ISBN-10: 098534959X

First Edition: May 2016

10 9 8 7 6 5 4 3 2 1

Editors: Letitia Carrington
Interior & Cover Design: Davida Baldwin (OddBalldsgn.com)
Cover Photo: Davida Baldwin

Printed in the United States of America

To my husband Julian Seay, everyday you tell me you love me and express how blessed you are to have me as your wife, your best friend and soul mate. And I want you to know that I will never get tired of hearing you say it. I also want you to know that I love you more than I have anyone else and that even though I'm Kiki Swinson to my fans, I'm Mrs. Seay at home! I love you baby! And I'm so happy that God brought us together! Now let's continue to build this EMPIRE! Kisses!

Don't Miss Out On These Other Titles:

Novella Collaborations:

Prologue

"**I** told you I was going to get you, didn't I?" I said, grinding my teeth together as I buried the barrel of the gun in the temple of her head. I was seething. I couldn't get the thought out of my mind how this bitch fucked my husband and helped destroy my marriage.

"Talk your shit now bitch! Remember when you told me that you weren't going to stop fucking Drake because he had enough dick for everyone?" I yelled at her as I applied more pressure to her head.

"I only said it because that's what he told me to say."

"Shut the fuck up lying!" I spat and smacked her across the head with the butt of the gun. She let out a loud scream. I hit her again. "Shut the fuck up before I shoot you now." I roared.

Sobbing uncontrollably, she pleaded for her life but in my mind it was too late. I figured with all the pain she caused me, this was what she deserved. Not only had she had an affair with my man, she publicized it at the nightclub, making a mockery out of me, which in turn caused me to have a miscarriage. I wanted my baby so bad. It felt good to have something growing inside of me that I knew would love me pass everything I was going through. It didn't matter that Drake wasn't treating me right. All that mattered was that I was going to finally have someone to love and knew that it would be reciprocated. But guess what? It didn't happen. My bundle of joy slipped away from me and now all parties involved will pay for it.

"Please Kim, I beg you to let me go. I promise I won't tell anyone about this. I won't call the cops. I will just leave here like nothing happened." She pleaded.

"Bitch I ain't letting you go nowhere. I'm going to finish you once and for all. You killed my baby and now I'm gonna send you on a one-way trip to hell." I huffed as I pulled back on the chamber.

"No! No! Please don't kill me! I don't wanna die!" she screamed. Her face looked swollen, it was saturated with her tears.

"It's too late for that. Just shut up and say a silent prayer to your God and hope He lets you in heaven, you fucking bitch!" I shouted. I couldn't take it anymore. The sight of her was making me sick to my stomach. She didn't deserve to be alive so I pulled the trigger. BOOM!

How It All Started

I was once a good girl. Kim Majors was my maiden name until I married the love of my life, Drake Weeks. We had everything. Money and freedom to go and come as we please. Being the owner of a lucrative, upscale night club, we were able to afford a million dollar penthouse with house staff, his and hers Ferraris and a flawless set of VVS1 diamond earrings, necklaces and a half a million dollar, five carat, cushion –cut diamond ring.

Life was great until the moment I hired a private investigator and found out that my husband was cheating on me with a rack of different women. So immediately after I left the P.I. 's office, I decided to confront my husband at the nightclub. But when I walked into his office and caught him nose-diving in one of this nightclub hostesses' pussy, I snapped. This bastard literally had this slut sitting on the edge of his office desk with her legs straddling his shoulders. I instantly saw red and went the fuck off! I grabbed that bitch by her hair and wrapped it around my hand as tight as I could and then I yanked her ass backwards.

She hit the floor hard. BOOM! From there I started stomping that ho in her face.

While I was kicking her ass my cowardly ass husband ran out of his office and left his bitch to fend for herself. He didn't leave her with me long, though. A few minutes later, he came rushing back in the office with a few guys from his security team. It took them about two whole minutes to pull me off that bitch, so by the time they pulled us apart, I had a ton of her weave in my hands and the top half of her dress wrapped around my wrist. I wanted that ho to feel my wrath and she did.

Later that night, I threw his shit out of our house and quickly hired a divorce attorney. After my attorney and I was done with Drake, I walked away with a $1.5 million dollar lump sum of cash, I got to keep all of my diamond jewelry and my car.

You would think that by walking away with a great severance package I would be happy, but guess what? I'm not. It's been six months since my divorce settlement and I can't move on. I've had over a dozen men with seven-figure bank accounts pursue me, but I won't give them the time of day. Why? Because I'm still bitter by the fact that I lost my husband to some of the most grimy ass bitches in my city. Every one of them knew my husband was married. But that didn't matter to them. They still entertained his ass and sucked his dick dry. And in the process, I got hurt, lost my baby and lost my fucking soul mate. But vengeance is mine and those hos are going to pay. One by one, I am going to fuck their lives up just like they did mine. The same private investigator I hired to snoop around on my husband gave me all the Intel I needed on each one of these hos.

The first bitch on my list was Sandy Pilar. She used to work for my ex-husband at the nightclub as his hostess. She's now working as a hostess for a five-star restaurant in the Pembroke area of Virginia Beach. She and her boyfriend Dominic Mitchell of eight months had just moved in a two-bedroom apartment in Norfolk. The apartment was low budget but it was perfect for her broke ass.

After reading all the information my private investigator had given me, I learned that Sandy left for work everyday at 4:00 pm. And minutes after, her boyfriend would come home from work for the day.

So, while I waited outside in my Ferrari for his arrival, I got a phone call from my best friend Mariah. "Hello," I said immediately after I connected the call.

"Where are you?" she wanted to know. Mariah was a sweetheart and she was beautiful inside and out but she was nosey as hell. She was my childhood friend, so she seen me go through all the drama that was thrown my way over the past few years.

Like me, Mariah was also a divorcee. But she had two children from her previous marriage and it's been hard on her because now the kids have to divide their time between her and her ex-husband William Slone. Not only that, she had to deal with the fact that her ex-husband married his mistress immediately after their divorced was finalized. That scandalous shit he did sent Mariah into deep depression and she's now finally getting over him, which was why I couldn't tell her what I had going on. She wouldn't approve of it and even worse, she'd probably think about her situation and fall back into depression.

"I just picked up some dinner from the Thai restaurant and now I'm getting ready to head home. Why? What's up?" I replied.

"The twins just came back from their father's house and told me that Tammy was mean to them while they were there. So, you know I wanna step to that bitch and tell her to check herself before I run up in there and whip her ass!"

"I wouldn't let you kick her ass because you know she'll get you locked up for that. But I'd call her and curse her out." I told her.

"You're right. But it would be fun to see that bitch get stretched out across the floor with a couple of black eyes." Mariah joked.

"Yes, it would." I agreed and chuckled.

"What are you doing tomorrow? Let's get together and do lunch." Mariah suggested.

"Sure let's do that. What time?" I said.

"How about 1:00?"

"Sounds great."

"Good. Because there's this new seafood restaurant on the ocean front and I'm dying to try them out."

"I'm there." I assured her.

Mariah and I talked for a few more minutes about life but when I saw movement through the left side of my peripheral vision, I immediately turn around and noticed that the guy from the photo provided by the P.I. took off running and started jogging away from the apartment building. "Hey Mariah, let me call you back." I rushed to say and disconnected our call before Mariah could utter another word.

I threw my cell phone down on the passenger seat and sped off into the road. I literally went from 0 to 60 miles per hour real quick. Halfway down the block I slowed down as I approached the 6'1, caramel complexion, brother with chiseled features and the ripples in his stomach to go with it. I could tell that he was at least five years younger than I was, but at this point it didn't matter. I wanted my revenge and he was the hot ticket item that would help me get it.

I pulled up beside him and cleared my throat so he could hear me. He turned his attention in my direction and I smiled on cue. "Please tell me you're a personal trainer, because I could sure use one right now." I said, seductively. I showed him my entire set of bleached white teeth.

He smiled back and his smile was radiant. His teeth were almost as white as mine. He had a freshly done Ceaser haircut that illuminated his sideburns, his mustache and his gold tee. This guy was the real deal. He'd definitely make Idris Elba take a seat. "No, I'm not a trainer. But I've done some training for a few of my female cousins." He finally said as he continued to jog slowly.

"Think I could tag along with you and your cousins the next time you guys workout?" I pressed the issue. I tossed him some bait hoping he'd take it.

"Maybe." He smiled once again.

"Please don't do that." I commented even though this was the reaction I wanted.

"Don't do what?"

"Don't smile. It's intoxicating."

"So is yours." He complimented me.

Thankfully, we were approaching a stoplight. I knew that this would be the perfect time to get him a little closer to me. I figured if he got a chance to look into my car and see what I was working with, he'd be more compelled to flirt a little more.

I stopped at the corner and so did he. "Come here so I can get a better look at you." I instructed him.

After he approached my car he looked me straight in the eyes. "Your eyes are beautiful." His compliments continued.

"Thank you." I replied and bit down softly on my bottom lip.

"Don't mention it."

"So, what's your name?" I asked him. He didn't need to know that I already knew the answer to this question. My main objective was to get him talking.

"Dominic. And yours?"

"Kim," I told him. "So, I take it you live nearby?"

He hesitated for a moment. I could tell that he wasn't certain about whether he wanted to divulge that information, so I figured now would be a good time to let him know that he could be honest with me. I grabbed his right hand with my left hand and pulled him towards me. I held his hand gently and said, "Look Dominic, I understand that you and I just met so it's okay if you wanna be careful. I mean, I could be a stalker." I giggled to make him feel easy.

"Nah, it ain't that," he said and then he fell silent as he looked around at his surroundings.

"Well, it must be that you have a wife," I blurted out.

"Nah, I'm not married. But I do have a girl." He said hesitantly.

"Do you two have any kids?"

"Nope," he said and took a step back from the car. He took another look around him.

"You must live fairly close because you're acting pretty nervous right now."

"Oh nah, I'm good. She's at work. It's just that I've got a lot of nosy ass neighbors."

"Well, if you want to, you could hop in my car and we can go somewhere where no one knows you. And who knows, you may get lucky while you're out." I smiled at him.

He looked at me suspiciously. "You aren't a cop are you?"

"No, silly. Come get in my car and let's go have a cocktail downtown." I encouraged him. "I'm not gonna bite you Dominic." I smiled again.

"Okay, I'll go with you this time but I want you to know that you're cutting into my running time." He smiled back as he walked around to the passenger side of my car.

"Don't worry. I'll make it up to you." I assured him.

"I'm gonna hold you to that." He told him after he sat down and closed the door.

I pulled back into the road and drove through the light after it turned green. The way I revved up my engine gave Dominic an instant hard on. "This is a nice ass car! How much did this bad boy set you back?"

"Nothing, but I'll make sure I ask my ex-husband the next time I speak with him."

"Oh my bad! Sorry to hear that." He tried apologizing.

"No need to apologize. I say good riddance."

"So, you're not seeing anyone?"

"No way."

"Why not? You're fucking gorgeous."

"Thank you."

"So, what do you do?"

"I own a few investment properties that give me a good return. What about you?"

He let out a long sigh and then he said, "Well, I work for my girlfriend's father doing landscaping work. And I fucking hate it."

"Why?"

"Because it gets really hot for one. So to deal with that and the fact that I work for an asshole is a recipe for a disaster."

"How long have you been working for this guy?"

"Four months now."

"Well, it can't be all that bad. I mean, at least you have job."

Yeah. Barely."

"Well, I guess taking a ride out to get a cocktail was a good idea after all." I commented and smiled.

The Yard House

I decided to take Dominic to the Yard House sports bar and restaurant for cocktail hour. On our way into the bar he complimented me on my sundress and the 4-inch, Jimmy Choo sandals I was wearing. I thanked him after he opened the door for me.

After I ordered our drinks we sat at the bar and talked our heads off. He was definitely a young guy at heart. It seemed like he was more interested in playing games on his Xbox One than talk about politics, so I learned fairly quickly that the only thing he and I had in common was that his girlfriend fucked my husband and I was going to fuck him. "Can you excuse me for a minute? Gotta' go and make a bathroom run." He said as he stood up from the sit at the bar.

"Can I join you?" I winked at him.

He looked around the bar and then he looked back at me. "You wanna go in the men's bathroom with me?"

"Yeah, if that's okay with you."

"What if someone's in there?"

"Then we'll wait until they come out." I told him.

"A'ight, well come on." He replied like a giddy little child.

I stood up from the barstool and followed him into the men's restroom. Thankfully no one was in the men's bathroom when he walked in. I let him handle his business while I locked the bathroom door. While his back was still facing me, I pulled out my iPhone, pressed the record button and placed it near the sink area where he wouldn't see it.

Immediately after he flushed the urinal he shook his dick off and proceeded towards me. I handed him a paper towel from the dispenser and then I leaned against the sink, giving my iPhone enough clearance to record every move Dominic made.

He smiled as he wiped his dick dry and dropped the paper towel in a nearby trashcan. "Are you sure you wanna do this?" he asked me.

"Of course I do." I assured him as I began to spread my legs. He cupped me into his arms and lifted me onto the sink. Without any warning he pulled my panties to the side and slid his fully erect dick inside of me. The sudden feel of his hard dick gave me butterflies. I exhaled with each stroke. "Ooooooohh, your pussy is so wet and sweet." He started off.

After twenty consecutive strokes Dominic had a steady rhythm going. His dick was good if I had to say so myself. "Fuck me Dominic! Fuck me!" I said loud enough for my recorder to catch it but soft enough that no one on the outside of the bathroom would hear.

"This dick is good ain't it?" he commented as he continued to gyrate his dick inside of me.

"Yes, it is." I managed to reply between strokes. The excitement behind the fact that he was pounding the hell out of my pussy sent chills up my spin. I went in with the discussion to fuck Dominic to hurt Pilar but after digging in his cookie jar, it made me rethink my motives. I couldn't figure out if I falling in love with this guy or lust because of the way he was fucking me. I was so fucking confused.

"Is this the best pussy you ever had?" I said loud enough for only he could hear me.

"Yes girl, this is the best pussy ever." He huffed like he was running out of breath.

After a total of sixty-three strokes his dick erupted. He pulled the head of his penis out before any of his cum could seep inside of me. I watched it ooze from the hole of penis as he massaged the shaft area. He held his head back like he was trying to regain his senses.

I snatched my phone up from the back of the sink and slid it down into my handbag so he wouldn't see it. After it was secure I stood up and fixed my panties and my dress while Dominic did the same. Luckily for us, the moment we decided to leave the bathroom was the exact same time another gentleman was trying to come in. Dominic greeted the guy while I giggled on my way out.

Back at the bar Dominic and I laughed and talked about everything around the sun. He had this way about him that was so infectious. I had only spent about an hour with him and could already see why Sandy fell in love with him.

Back At The Home Front

I dropped Dominic back off at the same corner I picked him up at and raced home. I took a long hot shower. While I let the hot water cascade down my back I kept replaying how good he fucked me in the men's bathroom. Just the mere thought of him penetrating me, gave me goose bumps and made my pussy tingle. I swear I hadn't had a man fuck me like that in a long time. I dared to tell Mariah about my rendezvous because she'd flip out and then as soon as I tell her how I bumped into him and who'd he belonged to. I wouldn't hear the end of it.

After I showered, I made myself a hot cup of tea and then I cuddled up on my bed, cradling my iPhone in my hands. I was itching to see the footage I had recorded earlier, especially after the way Dominic made me feel during our encounter. So, immediately after I pressed the play button I sunk deeper into pillow and watched intently at how good he fucked me.

"Oh yes, this dick feels good inside of me." I whined. "Please don't stop." I heard myself beg him while I watched the video. I was holding onto him for dear life.

I could see the expression on his face as clear as day. The way he looked at me while he plunged his dick inside of me, told me that he was thoroughly enjoying himself. I even caught him closing his eyes a few times like he envisioned that he and I were somewhere else. The passion he felt from my body oozed from his mouth as he gently bit me on my neck and shoulders. If I hadn't known any better I would say that this guy was falling head over heels for me.

The video footage of he and I lasted for four minutes. And it was a good four minutes. It was hot and steamy to say the least. I wanted to watch it all over again but I my coochie started getting moist so I left well enough alone.

After I sat my phone down on the bed next to me, I thought about how I was going to break the news to Sandy and show her the video. I knew I wanted to hurt her the way I got hurt behind my marriage. But I figured public humiliation wasn't going to be enough for me. I wanted to make that bitch's life a living hell! I wanted her to cry a bunch of nights like I did. And if by any chance she was pregnant, I wanted her to miscarry too. I just wanted her to beg for mercy by the time I was through with her ass. And that's what I intended to do.

I didn't realize that I had dozed off until my cell phone started ringing. I didn't bother to look at the caller I.D. because I didn't have a man and I only had one best friend so I knew it had to be her. I answered the call on the second ring. "Hello," I said.

"I can't stop thinking about you." I heard Dominic say.

Shocked by his voice, I had to take the phone away from my ear and look at the caller I.D. just to make sure it was him. "Dominic, is this you?" I asked.

"Of course it is. Who else would it be?" he replied.

"I'm just shocked to hear your voice." I told him.

"Well, I've been sitting here in my apartment and I can't stop thinking about you."

"That's a good think right?" I toyed with the question.

"It's bitter sweet."

"So, what are you going to do about it?" I continued to question him. I knew this nigga was falling for me and I loved every minute of it.

He sighed heavily. "I don't know."

"Where is your girlfriend?" I asked him even though I already knew where she was. For God's sake I had her work schedule.

"She's at work." He told me.

"What does she do?" I continued to question him.

"She's a hostess at a restaurant."

"Can I ask you a couple of personal questions?" I asked him, testing the waters.

"Sure. What's up?"

"How long have you two been together?"

"Close to eight months, I think."

"How long have you two been living together?"

"Not long."

"So do you see yourself marrying her one day?"

"After what happened between me and you today, getting married to her is the furthest thing from my mind." He replied.

It was refreshing to hear Dominic express the feelings he had developed from the sexual encounter we had earlier, but he was moving a little too fast for me. "Flattery will get you nowhere." I teased him, jokingly.

"I am really serious right now. I am crushing on you like a motherfucker! I wished I was with you right now." He expressed.

"Sounds like somebody's falling in love." I continued to tease him. Dominic was definitely a sweetheart. He was nice looking. He smelled good. And he even fucked good. But I wasn't on the market to take on a new relationship. All I wanted was revenge and I intended to get it, even if it meant to hurt Dominic's heart in the process. I mean, no one cared about my heart.

Dominic went on and on about how sexy and gorgeous I was and that he couldn't believe why I didn't belong to anyone. "Your husband was a damn fool to leave you!" He commented. "If I would've met you before I got into this relationship I'm in now, then I would've been over there with you instead of here."

"You sure do know how to put a smile on my face."

"Don't think I'm pulling your leg. I'm telling you some truthful shit right now." He said and then he paused for a second. "It's rare trying to find a woman like you. You got the total package."

"Yeah and sometimes having the total package intimidates men."

"Yeah, well it wouldn't intimidate me. 'Cause if you were my woman, I'd walk around town with a T-shirt on my back with your name and face printed on it and let the whole world know that you belong to me."

"Yeah, yeah, yeah. That's what they all say." I giggled.

"What are you doing tomorrow?"

"I'm not sure. Why?"

"Because I would love to see you again."

"Where do you want to meet up?"

"I would love to take you to my favorite Creole spot for lunch."

"Where is it?"

"Virginia Beach."

"What time?"

"I take my lunch at 1 o'clock. But will that be a good time for you?"

"Yes, I think I can make it."

"Okay, well I'm gonna text you the address and I'll see you tomorrow at 1pm."

"One it is." I said and then I disconnected our call.

Reality Check

I couldn't get Dominic off my mind after I hung up with him. One part of me was feeling him but the other part of me looked at him like all the other fucked up guys in the streets. Who cares if he's full of compliments and that he wishes that he'd never met Sandy because he'd be with me? At the end of the day he was fucking around on her. And I figured that if the shoe was on the other foot and I was his live-in girlfriend, he'd fuck around on me too. So, he gets treated like all the other niggas in the world. It's payback time!

Immediately after I hung up with Dominic I called my *go-to-guy*. He was the muscle behind my plans to destroy all of my ex-husband's *rebound bitches*. "Hey is this a good time to talk?" I asked him.

"Yeah, we're good. What's up?" he answered. I didn't have a name for him. I was instructed by my private investigator to refer to him as my Go-to-Guy. I'd only met him once in person. He was a very tall guy. He'd put you in the mind of the former Founder and CEO of Death Row Records, Suge Knight. He

24

wasn't cocky or flamboyant like Suge Knight. He was the complete opposite. He was a quiet and observant guy. But when you look into his eyes, you'd know that he was a coldblooded killer.

"I'm going on a lunch date tomorrow at 1:00, so I'm going to need you to get into position." I told him.

"Well, I'm going to call you back on my secured line. When I call back just give me the address and I'll take care of the rest."

"Okay." I replied.

Two seconds later the phone line went dead. My phone rang three seconds later. I answered it. "Hello," I said.

"Where is it?"

"394 Millstone Road. The apartment number is 12."

"Thank you." He said and then the phone went silent. And before I was able to ask if he was still on the other line, I heard the dial tone. Just like that, he was gone again.

Girl Talk

M y BFF Mariah rang my cell phone first thing in the morning. I was knocked out sleep when I heard my phone rang. I answered it on the second ring. "Girl, this better be important." I said, sounding groggy.

"Girl, you're not gonna believe the shit I am about to tell you." Mariah huffed. I instantly heard the irritation in her voice so I sat up in my bed.

"What happened?" I asked her.

"Girl, why my twins just told me that they heard Tammy and their dad having sex in their bedroom yesterday."

"You have got to be kidding?"

"No I am not. And I am pissed. What kind of shit they got going on over there that they can't act like responsible adults? Who fucks in the middle of the day?" Mariah spat.

"Adults that don't have kids."

"Exactly."

"So, what did they say? How did the conversation come up?" I wanted to know.

"Well, while we were eating breakfast Tasha was

26

watching a man and woman making out on YouTube, so I told her to turn that mess off. And she comes back at me and says, that it's not like she hasn't seen it before. So, I looked at her and asked her where she's seen it because it hadn't been at my home. And that's when she tells me that her and Tisha hears their dad and Tammy having sex all the time while they're over there."

"Get the fuck out of here! She said that?"

"Yes, she did."

"And where was Tisha when she said all that?"

"Sitting at the kitchen table with us. And before I could get the words out of my mouth, she confirmed it."

"Oh my God! So what are you going to do?"

"I'm gonna have a nice little chat with both of their asses! I don't play that mess! What kind of example are they setting for these girls? My babies are both 10 years old. They don't need to be hearing grown-ups fucking. It's bad enough that they are seeing that bullshit on TV."

"So where are the girls now?"

"I just dropped them off to school."

"Well, you need to be getting him on the phone right now."

"Oh don't worry. As soon as I hang up with you, I'm calling his ass!"

"Look I know you're upset, but just try not to argue with him. You know he'll find any reason to hang up on you. He may even deny that it happened."

"Well, I'll tell you what, if he gives me any lip behind this, I'm gonna call her ass! And he's not gonna want me to do that."

"You're right about that."

"Okay, well before I go, are we still on for our one o'clock lunch today?"

"Oh damn," I replied after I thought about the one o'clock plans I had with Dominic.

"What's wrong?"

"I'm gonna have to take a rain check on our lunch today. I forgot I had a doctor's appointment." I lied.

"Okay, that's cool. Call me later. Maybe we can have dinner."

"Okay thanks for understanding."

"You know I love you girl!"

"I love you too."

Our 2nd Date

I met Dominic a few hours later at his favorite restaurant. Surprisingly, he was already there with bell and whistles. He stood up from his seat as I approached him. He gave me a warm embrace and kissed me on the cheek. "You look and smell so good." He complimented me.

"Thank you." I replied and then I smiled while I took my seat on the bar stool next to him. I knew I was looking good. I purposely wore my brand new Versace print, wrap around dress showing my curves and major cleavage.

"I miss you so much." He expressed as he stared at me.

"What do you miss about me?" I quizzed him, stilling smiling.

"Come on now. Stop playing games with me. You know I'm feeling the hell out of you." He said.

"I'm……….." I started off but was quickly interrupted by the sudden ring of his cell phone.

"Excuse me, I gotta' take this." He told me and pressed the send button. "Hello," he said.

"Where are you?" I heard a woman's voice ask. I

immediately knew it was Sandy.

"I'm at the bar with one of my homeboys from work." He lied.

"Where at?" she continued to question him.

"Why?" He asked her. He was getting hotter around the collar by the second.

"Because I wanna come by and see you." She told him.

"Well, that won't be a good idea because I'm about to get out of here." He lied to her once more.

I heard her sighed heavily. "Well alright. I guess I'll go home then." She finally said.

"Where are you?" He wanted to know.

"I'm sitting outside in the parking lot of your job."

"Why didn't you call and tell me you were coming up to my job?"

"Because I wanted it to be a surprise. I picked up a couple of sandwiches from your favorite deli and I wanted you and I to sit in the car and eat it together."

"Well, I'm sorry. You should've called me."

"It's okay. I'll take the sandwiches home and leave yours in the microwave so you can eat it later."

"A'ight."

"I love you."

"I love you too." He assured her.

Several seconds after he disconnected their call, he laid his cell phone down on the bar area near his drink and continued on with our lunch date. "Sounds like you're being missed." I commented.

"Nah, it ain't like that. She's just a little to needy at times." He replied and then he quickly turned the focus back on me. We ordered a couple of drinks and two appetizers. When the food was brought over to us, he asked if he could feed me. Of course, I obliged.

Minutes into the eating and warming up to each other, he excused himself to go to the men's room. "Oh sure, go ahead." I told him.

I watched intently as he stood up from his chair and walked away from the bar. I held my breath hoping that he'd forget his cell phone. I swear I started talking underneath my breath. "Please, leave your phone. Please leave your phone." I said loud enough for only I could hear it. I even looked away and pretended to look at the big screen TV hanging from the ceiling across the bar to throw him off.

Seconds later, he headed in the direction of the restroom. This guy literally walked away and forgot his cell phone. I was beyond happy. But I knew that if I didn't grab it and put my plan into motion, then this moment would be wasted.

Before I grabbed his phone in my hand, I looked over my shoulder to see if he had entered the restroom. And when I saw that the coast was clear, I scrambled with the buttons of the keypad on my phone. "Come on now Kim, calm down and focus." I coached myself along.

Finally after a few keystrokes I was able to text a copy of the video footage of he and I fucking on the bathroom sink from the day before. After I heard his text message indicator beep, I grabbed his phone and went into his call log. It didn't take me long to find Sandy's cell phone number considering she had just called him. Without hesitation, I attached the video from his phone and forwarded to her cell phone. Immediately after I pressed the SEND button, I let out a long sigh. "Priceless!" I uttered quickly.

Before I laid his cell phone back down on the bar next to his drink, I deleted my text to his phone, and then I deleted the videotext that I forwarded from his cell phone to hers. I couldn't leave any traces of evidence that I leaked this video. And when I was done, I turned the ringer off.

After I laid his phone back down, I realized that as soon as she saw the video of us that she'd call him. And even though she wouldn't be able to get in touch with him now, she'd eventually find a way. So, without further thought, I tapped my glass of water with the back of my hands and knocked it over. All the water inside of it spilled onto Dominic's phone. "Oh shit! Can I get some extra napkins over here." I pretended to panic. I said it to draw attention to the bartender. I knew I was going to need a witness for accidentally spilling water on his cell phone.

"Oh man! What happened?" Dominic asked while he watched the bartender and I wipe the water up from the bar with paper towels. I had already placed his cell phone on top of a dry napkin.

"I'm so sorry. But I accidently knocked over my glass of water and it got on your phone." I said apologetically.

Dominic snatched his phone from the bar. He turned it over and over as he inspected it.

"If the water damaged it, then I'll replace it." I assured him.

"Don't worry about it. It should be okay." He told me.

"No. I insist." I pressed the issue.

"Nah, it's all good. If it's damaged then I'll take care of it." He replied.

"Are you sure?"

"Yes, I'm sure." He smiled and slid the phone into his front pants pocket.

After Dominic helped clean up the rest of the water, he looked down at this watch and realized that he had to head back to work. I gave him a kiss on his check and walked hand in hand to our cars in the nearby parking lot. "Damn I wished I didn't have to go back to work. It's like I can't get enough of you." He commented as he looked at me from head to toe.

I smiled bashfully. "Stop it. You're making me smile." I lied. I really wasn't feeling him like I was letting on. I needed him to help me execute my plans to destroy his bitch. So, if that meant to lead this dummy on, then so be it.

I hopped in my car and watched Mr. Dominic as he drove away. I knew this would be the last time I saw him. Bon Voyage! I said. It was barely audible. But it felt good saying it.

My Alibi

I called my best friend Mariah. I needed someone to talk to so I could get my mind off what was about to go down. I Face Timed her. "What are you doing?" I asked her.

"I'm at the mall looking for something to wear to my cousin's baby shower this coming weekend."

"Did you have at talk with that bitch yet?"

"I tried to call both of them right after I hung up with you but neither one of them answered their phones."

"I would've text them."

"I did that too. But they haven't responded."

"Sounds like you're gonna have to take a trip over to their house." I suggested.

"I'm already ahead of you. After I leave the mall, I'm heading straight there."

"Have you thought about what you're going to say?"

"You know I have."

"Well have you thought about the fact that they may tell you to mind your business?"

"I wish they would. I swear Kim, I'll go the fuck

off on them both if they came out their mouths with some fly shit like that."

"I know you will. But please keep in mind that if you go over there with those intentions, you'll be giving them the power over you. Not only that, they're going to press charges against you. And before you know it, you'll be pulled in a circle of drama."

"Kim, I would never let them get that much power of me."

"Look Mariah, I'm not trying to tell you what to do. All I'm saying is to be smart about it. There's plenty of ways to get back at them."

"Well, I'm all ears." Mariah replied sarcastically.

"How long are you going to be at the mall?"

"For another 20 minutes, why?"

"Because I feel like you're gonna need me around when you make this trip to your ex- husband's house."

"You might be right. So, meet me at the food court by 2:30."

"See you in a second." I told her.

I hopped back in my car and headed up to the mall to meet Mariah. I finally met up with her in the food court. She looked very fashionable. I've always called her a fashionista. She seldom wore anything that wasn't labeled D & G, Fendi, Ferrogamo or Chanel. She was a high-end shopper to the tenth power. So, it was kind of weird to see her carrying a shopping bag from Macy's. I looked at her strange. "You bought something out of Macy's?" I asked her.

She took a sip from her Chick-fil-a cup and after she swallowed her beverage, she said, "They had a sale on wine glasses so I picked up a couple of sets."

"Did you find anything to wear?"

Mariah sighed heavily. "Nope. I'm just gonna pull something out of my closet."

"Good. Now let's get out of here." I said.

Mariah and I headed back out to the parking garage. She got into her car and I got into mine. I followed her uptown to the area where her husband shared a cozy new home with his new wife. When we pulled up curbside to the house Mariah and I noticed that both cars were there. Mariah got out of her car first. I followed suit. "You see both of these clowns are here, right?" Mariah commented sarcastically as she stormed up the driveway.

I scurried up the driveway behind her. "Please calm down before this visit takes a turn for the worst." I advised her.

"I'm calm. But somebody is gonna answer my questions today." Mariah warned me.

Before Mariah and I could put one foot on the steps that lead to the front door, the door opened and out pops Mariah's ex-husband's head. "What are you doing here?" he asked Mariah. The stare William gave her sent chills down my back. He made no secret that he didn't want her there.

"I came here because we need to talk."

"About what?" he replied. He was very short with her.

"William don't play stupid with me. I've been calling you and Tammy both so we can talk about when the girls come over for weekend visits they always seem to hear you and Tammy fucking like wild horses in your bedroom."

"That's bullshit! That has never happened. You're making that up." He snapped.

"No she's not William. I was there when one of the twins told Mariah." I interjected. I was lying through my teeth. But I had jump to my best friend's defense because he wasn't taking any slack off her.

"Who asked you?" he spat.

"Yeah, who the hell gave you permission to speak?" Tammy spoke as she reared her head around William's shoulders.

"And who gave you permission to speak?" I snapped. "Bitch you don't know me! I will take your fucking head off and won't even feel bad about it after I do it. So, you better stay in your lane." I warned her.

Tammy tried to step on the porch but William

detained her by grabbing her around the waist and pulling her back. "Let it go Tammy, these bitches aren't even worth it." He huffed.

"Don't hold her back. Let her ass go. I've been wanting to kick her ass since she fucked up our marriage." Mariah roared.

"Just get off our property before I called the cops on you." William threatened.

"I'm not going anywhere until we address this issue." Mariah retorted.

"What part of it didn't happen don't you understand?" William hissed.

"So, you're telling me that our kids made that shit up?"

"No bitch! You made it up!" Tammy interjected.

Without warning Mariah leaped onto the porch where Tammy and William was standing in a matter of seconds. She lunged back and threw a punch. From the direction Mariah was aiming, I could tell that it was meant for Tammy. Fortunately for Tammy, William blocked it. He took the blow to the right side of his face. After he realized that he was hit, he grabbed her by her neck with his right hand and I sprang into action.

I ran up the steps and tried to pry his hand from around Mariah's neck. She started coughing and gagging instantly. "Let her go William. This is not the way to handle things." I told him while I concentrated on pulling back one of his fingers at a time.

"I'm calling the cops." Tammy belted out and then she dashed back into the house.

I looked into Mariah's eyes and realized that she was slipping into unconsciousness. Her face started turning blue as William began to suck the life out of her. "Come on William, please let her go. You're gonna kill her." I begged.

Mariah gagging and coughing started happening less frequently. Fear engulfed my entire body. I knew that if I didn't something to stop him, then I'd be attending my best friend's funeral.

Out of nowhere a guy rushed up from behind me. He startled me when he jumped onto the porch. But when I saw him grab William by his arm and hand, and told him to let Mariah go, I knew he was a guardian angel. "Let her go William. It's not worth it brother." The guy spoke.

It took another couple of seconds for the guy to convince William, but he finally persuaded William into releasing the chokehold he had on Mariah. Immediately after he let her go, I grabbed Mariah into my arms.

I don't know how I did it, but I carried her down the steps while she tried to catch her breath. She coughed nonstop. "Mariah, I know your throat hurts so try to breath slow." I coached her.

While I was putting her in the passenger side of my car, two police squad cars with two police officers in each car sped on the scene. The way they parked their cars blocked me from trying to leave.

It didn't surprise me to see that all four cops were white. The neighborhood William lived in was a very posh community. Two of the officers approached Mariah and I while the other two officers walked over to speak with William. By this time, Tammy had come back out of the house. The guy who convinced William to let Mariah go stood there alongside both of them as the cops approached them.

"Is she alright?" One of the officers asked.

"I'm not sure. She might need a paramedic to look at her." I suggested.

"What happened to her?" The other officer asked.

"She came over here to talk to her ex-husband about a matter that effected their kids, but he didn't want to talk. Instead, he tried to choke the life out of her." I explained.

"Is that true ma'am?" The second officer asked, while the other officer dispatched paramedics.

"Yes," Mariah finally spoke. It was barely audible.

"Did you hit him first?" He wanted to know.

"No, she didn't." I interjected. I knew that if Mariah had answered his question, she'd tell him the truth. And I wasn't having that. I hated William for how he played Mariah. So, it would make me warm and fuzzy to see that bastard get locked up.

"What is your name?" The officer's questions continued.

"Mariah Slone." She told him, her words were still barely audible.

"A paramedic will be here in a few minutes." The other police officer told us.

A few seconds later, both officers joined the other police officers that was questioning William and Tammy. Mariah and I both watched them explain their side of the story. "He's probably over there lying." I said.

Mariah nodded as if she agreed with me.

"It's alright because before we leave here today, I'm going to make sure he gets hauled out of here in handcuffs." I spat.

While all four officers talked to William and Tammy, the paramedics came on the scene. They asked Mariah a series of questions while they put hot compresses around her neck. They even checked her blood pressure. After they looked her over fully, they assured her that she would be fine. "You're gonna have some bruising for the next couple of days. And maybe even some swelling, but you'll be fine." One of the paramedics told her. We were relieved to know that she'd bounce back quickly.

I started getting Mariah situated in my car because I knew that I'd have to take her home, so after I buckled her down in the seatbelt and closed the passenger side door, the same two police officers that talked to us upon their arrival started walking back into our direction. I stood by the passenger side door and waited for them to approach us. Immediately after they came within two feet of Mariah and I the police officer that called the paramedic spoke first. "Well, Officer Reynolds and I just spoke with Mr. Slone and his wife and from what we were told, you Ms. Slone threw the first punch."

"That's a lie! They are lying!" I roared. Mariah sat there speechless.

"I'm sorry but the neighbor corroborated Mr. and Mrs. Slone's story. He said he was raking up the leaves in his front yard when everything happened. He even said that he was the one that talked Mr. Slone into letting you go after you hit him." The same officer continued to say.

"Officers they are lying. She didn't touch that man." I argued.

"We're sorry. But we're gonna have to take her downtown and charge her with assault and battery." The other officer chimed in as he leaned forward and opened the passenger side door of my car.

Both officers helped Mariah out of my car. I was broken hearted when I saw her drop a teardrop from her eye. I swear I felt her pain. But I knew I couldn't show any weakness, so I held back my tears and assured her that I was going to follow the cops down to the precinct so I could bail her out. "I'm right behind you Mariah." I said while I watched the officers handcuff and put her in the back of their squad car.

After they closed the door on her, I looked back at William and Tammy who were still standing on the porch with their neighbor. I gave them he nastiest facial expression I could muster up. "You're a really fucked up individual William. I just want you to know that." I yelled from my car.

"Just get the hell off my property before I have you arrested for trespassing." He yelled back.

"Fuck you! Get me arrested! I'm not afraid of you. You're a fucking woman beater for Christ's sake." I roared. My blood was boiling.

One of the police officers started walking towards me, while the other one stayed behind. I knew he was going to tell me to leave the premises so I got into my car before he could get within a couple of feet of me.

By the time I started the ignition he had made it to the curb. "Don't worry officer, I'm leaving right now." I told him and then I sped off.

Never Saw It Coming

I went straight to the police precinct so I could bail Mariah out of jail. Immediately after I entered into the lobby of the building I was instructed by the police officer behind the bullet proof window to have a seat because Mariah hadn't been processed as of yet.

Pissed off at the fact that Mariah or I shouldn't be here I stormed off to a set of chair and sat in one. I looked down at my watch and noticed that two hours had passed since I first met up with Mariah at the mall. I was so tired and promised myself that as soon as Mariah was released that I was going to go home and retire for the night.

Regrettably for me, I had to wait an additional two hours before Mariah was released from custody. Thankfully the magistrate judge released her on her own recognizance. She was so happy to see me waiting for her in the lobby area. She raced over to me and hugged me. Her embrace was strong. I could tell that she didn't want to let me go. And when she started crying all over again, I knew she was still hurt behind her arrest. I rubbed her back in a circular motion and started talking to her softly. "Stop crying. Everything's going to be alright." I told her.

Mariah lifted her head up from my shoulder and looked me directly in the eyes. "I called my mother to tell her that I needed her to pick the girls up from school but they weren't there when she got there. So, I told her to go over to William's house to get them but he refused to let the girls go, saying that he took out a retraining order against me because I was violent and that he feared for the safety of our girls."

"Are you fucking kidding me?" I snapped.

"That's not it."

"It gets worse." She started off. "My mother said he had my car towed away from his house." She continued.

"That low down motherfucker!" I spat. I couldn't believe what I was hearing. This motherfucker really went to great depths to ruin my best friend. But I wasn't going to let him get away with it. He was going to pay for this bullshit!

"Come on let's get out of here. We've got some phone calls that we need to make." I told her and escorted her towards the front door of the lobby.

As we were leaving a male and a female police officer announced that they were bringing in a suspect after they opened the glass door. "Please clear the way." They instructed everyone inside the lobby. That included Mariah and myself so we stood alongside the wall. When the officers saw that there was a clear path, they proceeded into the lobby area. It seemed like they were walking in slow motion after Sandy Pilar's eyes locked with mine. My heart dropped. Anxiety filled my entire body up while I watched the police officer escort her in handcuffs. I wanted to say something but my mouth wouldn't move. That didn't stop her though.

"That's her. That's the bitch that was fucking my boyfriend in that video. She probably knows who killed him." She began to scream as she stopped in her tracks. Unfortunately for her, she wasn't strong enough to hold her ground so they grabbed a tighter hold on her and forced her onto a nearby elevator.

"Isn't that one of girls that had an affair with Drake?" Mariah managed to say.

"Yeah, it was." I admitted.

"Well, what was she talking about? What does she mean you're the one who was fucking her boyfriend?" Mariah's questions continued.

"I don't know what the hell that crazy bitch is talking about."

"Well, whoever she's talking about apparently killed her boyfriend."

"Yeah, I guess." I replied nonchalantly and turned to leave. I pulled onto Mariah's arm as I walked off.

Right after Mariah and I got into my car I sped away from the police precinct with the biggest grin I could make. My plan had worked. "One down, five more to go." I mumbled underneath my breath.

"You say something?" Mariah asked me.

"It was nothing really. Just reminding myself about all the stuff I had to do in the next several days." I explained.

Mariah didn't say another word. She stared out the passenger side window as we passed other cars. I knew she wondered how she was going to get herself out of this jam. But I had already figured it out for her. Her problem was solved and it will be eliminated sooner than she thinks.

First Mission Completed

I finally talked Mariah into coming to my house after we left the police precinct. She reluctantly agreed to stay with me because she didn't want to go home and be alone. Five minutes after we arrived at the house Mariah decided that she wanted to lie down on my sofa so I gave her a blanket and turned on the television. I went into the kitchen to fix her a cup of hot tea and while I was grabbing the box of green tea from my kitchen cabinet Mariah yelled my name. She startled the crap out of me. I dropped the box of tea packets on the countertop and raced into the living room where she was. "What's the matter?" I asked in an alarming way.

"Look," she managed to say as she pointed towards the TV.

I immediately turned around and saw that she was looking at the news broadcast. I zoomed in and listened intently. "I'm standing on one of the busiest streets in Norfolk where a homicide has taken place." The black female news reporter started off. "It appears as though, there was a love quarrel and the male in this love triangle was murdered. No word on how the male

49

victim was killed. And police have yet to release his name but I can tell you that the murder suspect's name in this case is Sandy Pilar and she's being held in the Norfolk County Jail with no bail." The reporter continued.

The mere sight of Sandy Pilar's apartment gave me chills. Only I and one other person knew what went on there earlier today. And as far as I could tell, he definitely did his job. Dominic Mitchell was dead and Sandy Pilar's ass was behind bars and I want nothing else but for that bitch to rot in there too. What better place for her to think about how she fucked up my life?

After the reporter brought her report to a close Mariah turned down the volume with the TV remote and turned her attention towards me. "Isn't it weird that we just saw her down at the police precinct and now we actually know what she did?" Mariah asked.

"Yeah, that's crazy!" I commented.

"I wonder why she pointed you out and starting yelling that you were the one in the video with her boy friend?"

"I wondered the same thing." I replied in a causally. Then I quickly changed the subject. "So, have you thought about how you wanted to handle the situation with your ex-husband?"

Mariah let out a long sigh. "I'm gonna call my divorce attorney first thing in the morning. She'll know exactly what to do."

"You think she'll be able to handle the assault charge too?" I wondered aloud.

"Yeah, she handles all domestic and family issues." Mariah explained.

"Well then you should be good." I replied nonchalantly. But in reality, I really wanted to do things my way. Having her attorney fight her battles with her ex-husband in court was going to take forever. And knowing how fragile Mariah was, she was going to fall apart. Which was why, I needed to call in reinforcements. My guy would take care of her problem immediately. No questions asked.

Mariah and I talked a little more extensively about her plans to get her children back. I saw the pain in her face while she thought about the possibility that it may be a while before she saw them again, especially since her ex-husband filed a retraining order against her. I was beginning to find it very difficult to watch her wallow in her despair.

I loved Mariah like she was my own flesh and blood. She gave her ex-husband over 10 years of her life and this was the thanks she got. But I refuse to stand by and watch my friend cry her poor heart out behind a bitch ass nigga. I'd see his ass in a casket first. That's my word!

More Bad News

I had a very hard time sleeping last night. The thought of Dominic getting killed just so I could get rid of his bitch started to weigh heavily on me for some reason. I mean he really was a sweetheart. He damn sure knew how to fuck the shit out of me too. His conversations weren't that bad either. So, I see now why I'm feeling kind of fucked up inside about his demise. But then of course, his bitch Sandy Pilar rears her face and I immediately go back into *fuck the whole word* mode. No one care about my marriage or my unborn child so I hope that bitch rots in hell.

Before I hopped into the shower I went into the living room to check up on Mariah. When I entered into the living room I noticed that she was on her cell phone. She was covering her eyes with one hand while she held her phone against her ear with the other hand. "Are you alright?" I whispered, but it was loud enough for only her to hear me.

She immediately looked up and that's when I noticed the tears falling from her eyes. "Oh my God!

What's wrong?" I asked her, as I spoke a little louder while I took a seat on the sofa next to her.

"So, you're actually telling me that there's a possibility that I won't see my girls for at least 21 days?" Mariah questioned the caller, then she fell silent.

"Who are you talking to?" I whispered.

Instead of responding to my question, she took the phone away from her ear and placed the other caller on speaker so I could hear the entire conversation. "I'm sorry Mariah but my hands are tied until I hear back from the judge." I heard a woman's voice say. I knew then that Mariah was talking to her divorce attorney.

"How long do you think that would take?" Mariah asked. I heard mere desperation in her voice.

"It can take anywhere from now until the end of next week. Maybe even longer." Her attorney replied.

"I'm not gonna be able to go that long without seeing my kids! Who does he think he is? He can't do that. He can't keep them away from me. I'm their mother!" Mariah cried out. The pain in her voice magnified the entire living room area of my home.

"Listen Mariah, I know it's easier said than done, but you're gonna have to be strong. Twenty-one days may sound like a long time, but I've represented clients that had to wait longer than that to see their children."

"But I didn't do anything wrong! My ex-husband is just being a fucking dick head!" Mariah snapped.

The attorney let out a long sigh. "All I can say is if I hear from the judge sooner than I will give you a call."

Mariah didn't utter another word. She dropped her cell phone onto the floor so; I picked it up and pressed the END button without giving the attorney the heads up. Immediately after I disconnected the call, I placed the phone down on the coffee table in front of me and wrapped my arms around Mariah as she sobbed uncontrollably. She buried her head against my chest. "Why is he doing this to me?" she cried.

"Because he's an asshole, that's why?" I replied sarcastically while I rubbed her back.

"But I didn't ask for this. All I wanted to do was talk to him about the girls. That's it. And this is the thanks I get." Mariah continued to sob.

"You can't reason with irrational people Mariah. He's miserable. And he's unhappy with his life, which is why he's taking you through this bullshit! But it's going to be all right. You're gonna see your girls again sooner than you think." I told her. I was trying everything within my power to lift up her spirits.

I held her and talked to her for at least another ten minutes and finally she calmed down. Mariah wasn't build like me. She was a mild mannered woman with a sweet heart. To see her hurt, hurt me tremendously and I didn't like that one bit. But then I figured that William will get his soon enough. And I can't wait until Mariah can sit back and witness it.

After I helped Mariah come to terms with her situation, I made her a cup of hot tea and then I excused myself so I could jump in the shower. I took a long hot shower. It relaxed me so much that I didn't want to get out. But eventually I did.

On my way out of the bathroom, covered in my terrycloth robe, I went back into the living room to check on Mariah. I was hoping that she was feeling just a little better than she was after she had the talk with her attorney. I was also hoping that she would want to take a ride out with me this morning just so she could get some fresh air. It would be a great way for her to clear her head.

"Mariah honey, I'm gonna need you to go jump in the shower and freshen up so we can take a nice, long drove around the city." I said as I entered into the living room.

To my surprise she wasn't in there. So, I walked to the kitchen. I figured she was probably in there pouring herself another cup of tea. "Hey girl, did you hear me?" I asked as I stepped crossed the threshold of the entryway to the kitchen.

Once again, she was nowhere in sight. I turned around and exited the kitchen. "Mariah, where are you?" I yelled. But I got no answer. My place was pretty small in comparison to the home I once lived in with my ex-husband, but I had two more rooms to look into and that's where I headed. I looked into laundry room first since that was on my way to the guest room. And like I figured, she wasn't in there. So, then I headed to the guest room. There was no doubt in my mind that she wasn't in there considering that this was the last place in my house that she could be.

The door was slightly ajar so I pushed it open and to my surprise Mariah was nowhere in sight. Puzzled, I uttered the words, "Mariah where the fuck are you?" And when I didn't get an answer back, I shut the guest room door. BOOM!

Startled by the sudden CLUNK sound that came from the bedroom, I pushed the door back open and saw Mariah's lifeless body lying on the floor near the closet with one of my belts tied around her neck. In shear panic, I rushed to her side. "Oh my God! No Mariah, please don't tell me you did this. Please wake up." I cried out while I rushed to untie the belt from around her neck. "Please wake up Mariah! Don't do this to yourself. It's going to get better. I promise." I continued to sob while I pulled her into my arms.

I wrestled with Mariah's motionless body so that I

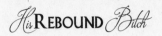

could perform CPR. I had no idea how long she had been like this but at this point it didn't matter because I started pressing down on her chest anyway. "Come on Mariah, come back to me girl. You have little girls that need you." I said after I breathed into her mouth.

I continued to perform CPR on Mariah for over four consecutive minutes but she wouldn't come back to me. Without even thinking about it, I started pressing down on her chest with all the strength I had while I cried out to her. "Mariah, please wake back up!" I screamed. "I need you here." I continued to ball uncontrollably because I knew she wasn't coming back.

Coming to terms that my best friend had just taken her own life wasn't something I was ready for. While I cradled her in my arms, I rocked her back and forth as the tears continued to fall from my eyes. I tried wiping the tears from my face but it didn't matter because they kept coming back. It didn't help that I found her suicide note in the top pocket of the shirt she was wearing while I was holding her in my arms. I immediately snatched it away from her body and unfolded it.

She had only written a few sentences but her words were powerful. I could tell that she had been hurting behind her divorce for a long time now.

Kim when you find this letter, I will already be dead. Now I don't want you to be sad because I going to a better place where I will never ever hurt again. Please tell my girls that I love them and that I will always be with them in spirit anytime they need to talk. I love you Kim. And please promise me that you will always be in my girl's lives. I don't care how you do it, but just don't let William shut you out. My babies need you.

Love always, your best friend Mariah.

Reading Mariah's last requests sunk me into a state of depression. I mean, how can she say that she's going to a better place? As bad as I want to be wrong, I've always been told that when a person commits suicide, they're going to hell. So, where is this place that she thinks is better than here? Not to mention, that fact that she wants me to be in her kids' lives. I knew William was going to fight me in court to prevent them from seeing me, but then I figured that if he were dead, then I wouldn't have that problem. I guessed, now is the time to set some things in motion.

My Next Move

I finally got up the courage to call the paramedics. So when everyone got here, homicide detectives surrounded me while I watched the coroners take Mariah's body out of my house. One of the detectives asked me if there was a suicide note, but I lied and told him no. But I did however, bring he and his partner up to speed about all of the events that led up to Mariah taking her own life, the female detective named Patricia Bowers handed me a business card to a Chaplain her department has partnered with. I took the card and dropped it on the coffee table in my living room. "If you need anything please don't hesitate to give me a call." She insisted.

"I won't." I replied nonchalantly and then I buried my head into both palms of my hands. "Oh yeah, are you guys going to get in touch with Mariah's mother?" I blurted out.

"Yes, we're going to take care of that." The detective assured me.

"Thank you." I replied, it was barely audible and then the detective walked off.

I swear it seemed like forever that the cops were at my home. So, when I looked at the time on my kitchen clock and realized that three hours had gone by, I completely flipped out. "I'm gonna need all of y'all to hurry up and get the hell out of my house. You've been here for far too long. My best friend's body has already gone out of here but y'all are still here. What's up with that? Am I missing something?" I yelled and screamed. Everyone started looking at me like I was fucking crazy but that didn't matter because I wanted them to think that I was crazy so they could get the fuck out of my house.

One of the uniformed police officers stepped up to me and assured me that they will all be vacating my premises in the next few minutes. He also apologized to me for losing Mariah.

Instead of feeding into his hollow ass condolences, I walked away from him and headed into my bedroom so I could get dressed. I needed to get out of my house before I lost my mind. I also needed to leave my house because I needed to make a very important phone call. I needed to get my enforcer on the line so I could give him instructions for my next kill.

An Hour & A Half Later

O nce the last forensic officer left I was able to leave the house. Immediately after I locked my front door I hopped in my car and headed down to the coffee shop down in Town Center of Virginia Beach. I had to come down to this part of town for two reasons. The first one was that I needed to check on my next victim's vehicle. And two, I needed to scout out the area so my go-to-guy wouldn't run into any interferences.

I purposefully drove into the parking garage because that's where my next victim always parked her car. I needed to make sure that she was at work so my hit could be executed.

While I was looking for a parking space for my car, I spotted her light gold color Honda Civic was parked on the third floor of the West side of the garage. "Glad to know that her dumb ass is at work today." I commented while I gritted my teeth. She was another bitch that I wanted eliminated really bad. She was one of the hos that wouldn't stop fucking my ex-husband Drake if I paid her to. She was fucking obsessed with him. She called our house all times of the night and that bitch had the nerve to take pictures of his dick with her cell phone and text them to me after she fucked him too death and put him to sleep. The nerve of her, right? Well I'll tell you what, that part of my life was the worse time for me. I hated everyone around me. I even hated myself for putting up with Drake's shit. But guess what? All of that is behind me now. And now I can relish in this moment until everyone has been dealt with. It was simple as that.

It was lunchtime for the city workers so I had to travel all the way up to the top floor of the parking garage just to get a parking space. Thankfully it wasn't raining. I took the elevator down to the first floor. And as soon as I walked off of the elevator I started dialing my contact guy at that moment. He answered on the first ring. "Is this a good time?" I asked him.

"Yes, but let me call you from the secure line." He said. And without giving me a chance to say okay, he disconnected our call. Two seconds later my cell phone rang. "Hello," I said.

"What can I help you with?" He got straight to the point.

"I've got another job for you." I told him.

"When do you need it done?" He wanted to know.

"A.S.A.P."

"You know the drill. Send me the address and the name of the job and I'll take it from there."

"What about the money?"

"Drop it off the same way you did the last time."

"Will do." I told him.

"Are you ready for the next faze of this operation?"

"Yes. I saw the vehicle and it's parked on the third floor." I said.

"Thanks for the info." He replied and then the line went radio silent.

My enforcer had every one of my ex-husband's mistresses' name, home addresses and work schedules on hand from the very first time he and I had met. At that meeting I also paid him in full for his services. Unfortunately he didn't have Mariah's ex-husband's information, which would require me to do some leg work by getting a few photo shots of him, and his daily schedule. I also knew that I had to get a few photo shots of his new wife Tammy and her work schedule as well. This guy didn't play any games when it came to executing his victims. He was very precise in every move he made and he doesn't take any hostages. So, if a person posed a threat to him, he would eliminate them on the spot.

In addition to getting him the information he needed, I also had to get him his money. His fee for his services was $20,000 per person, so I had to make a run to the bank, pull the money from my safe deposit box and then drop the cold hard cash off to a mail slot off an abandon warehouse across town. I dreaded every minute of it. But this move was necessary because it involved Mariah so it had to be done.

As planned I got myself a cup of hot coffee and a Biscoff cookie and took a seat outside at one of the curbside tables. I sipped on my coffee and played around with the Biscoff cookie because I really didn't have the appetite to eat it. I tried not to think about Mariah's death but my mind just wouldn't let me. The thought of losing her hurt my heart so bad. She was like a sister to me. We've been through everything together, so how was I going to manage not talking to her over the telephone anymore? And how was I going to have lunch dates or continue going to our Pilates classes without her? I knew that moving forward was going to be extremely hard for me. But more importantly, it was going to be hard for her girls too. I knew that once they heard the news about Mariah, they were going to be very sad. And just the mere thought that their no good ass father was going to have sole custody of them wasn't sitting right with me. I knew Mariah would turn over in her grave if I allowed that nigga to keep them. So, I couldn't let her down. Not then, and not now.

Doing Shit The Illegal Way

Like clockwork my next victim named Melissa Carson came strolling her ass out of her place of employment like she was the happiest person in the world. She had some other chick accompany her. I could tell that they were on their way to lunch because Melissa always parked her car in the parking garage and she was walking in the opposite direction of it. So after walking half way down the block she and her co-worker stopped at the Bahama Breeze restaurant and went inside.

I sat outside at the sidewalk table until I finished my coffee and when I was finally done, I paid the waitress and headed up the block so I could get a closer look at this Melissa chick. From the photos taken by the private investigator, she wasn't all that pretty looking in the face. But I will admit that she had the body of a video vixen and I'm sure that was what caught Drake's eyes when he initially hired her. She kind of resembled the African Actress Lupita Nyong'o. Besides that, the bitch didn't have shit on me. I was a bad bitch! And most recently I've become a *Rebound Bitch* and I am cool with that. Believe it or not, my ex-husband made me this way. And for me, there was no turning back. I vowed to get every last one of those hos that fucked my ex-husband so they'd better run for cover because I'm coming.

I had no intentions on staying long after I went inside of the restaurant. I took a seat at the bar and ordered their signature Bahama Breeze drink but without the alcohol. I even ordered their house salad to make it appear that I was actually a patron.

I noticed Melissa and her friend sitting in a booth five feet away from me. We were pretty close in proximity. So, when I heard the laughing and giggling and lips locking, I had to look up to see what was going on. I wasn't ready when I saw these two chicks kissing like their minds were going bad. Oh my God! These two bitches were lovers. I couldn't believe it. Who would've known?

Seething at the mouth, I had to count to ten in my head. Why the fuck was she fucking my ex-husband when the bitch was playing for the other side of the team? Talk about being selfish and confused.

After witnessing this bitch fondle and play kissy face with her fucking girl friend for the next thirty minutes I figured I had had enough and got up from the bar and headed back to my car.

It didn't take me long to get back to the parking garage. I was in and out of there in less than four minutes. So as I exited the garage out of nowhere comes this tall, statured, white guy dressed in all dark blue clothing, a fitted ball cap and dark sunshades with a backpack thrown over his left shoulder. He didn't look up but I knew he was my guy. So I wondered if he'd saw me? I do know that his presence was a bit frightening. He actually spooked the hell out of me when he walked by my car. I was glad that he was employed by me and not anyone else. The thought of him coming after me because someone paid him to do it, gave me an eerie feeling. Thank God for His protection.

As bad as I wanted to follow the guy so I could see him in action, I knew it was a bad idea and drove away from the garage. And besides, I had a job to do. Getting photos of Mariah's ex-husband and his wife had just become priority number one. So, I hopped on the highway and headed down Highway 264-East.

I knew William's office was located downtown Norfolk. He was a big time Accountant and had a firm in the Bank of America building on Waterside Drive. There was no way I would've been able to sit outside that building and wait for him to exit for the day. It was too congested. So, I parked my car and went inside the building to see him. I figured paying him a visit to discuss Mariah's death would be the perfect way to confront him without him becoming suspicious.

"Good afternoon ma'am and welcome to Charter Accounting Firm." The black woman greeted me as I approached the front desk in the lobby.

"Thank you. Is William available?" I asked her.

"No, he's not. I'm afraid he's in a meeting right now."

"How long do you think he's going to be in that meeting?" I questioned her.

"I'm sorry. But did you have an appointment with him? She quizzed me.

"No, I didn't. I'm his ex-wife's best friend and I have something very important to speak with him about." I explained.

"Well, what I can do is take down your name and number and have him call you back because I don't know how long he's going to be in that meeting." She said.

"I'll just wait," I told her. And then I sat down in one of the chairs in the waiting area. I pulled out my iPhone and started sifting through old text message while I waited for William's conniving ass to come out of his meeting. I started rehearsing in my mind what I was going to say to the nigga when I saw him. I wanted everything to come out right. I even wanted him to have a better attitude especially since we both lost someone that was near and dear to our hearts.

Mariah was an angel in my mind. She was the nicest and most loyal person a friend could have. She treated me like I was her sister. And when she was married to that jackass, she treated him like royalty. But I guessed that wasn't enough because after all the time and work she put into their marriage, he had to go out and fuck around her. So, how was Mariah supposed to act after finding that out? What, just let him get away with it? Hell no! Which was why she called all of his male clients and told them that he was fucking their wives. William lost like 30% of his business behind that one phone call. And because of it, he filed for divorce and left her. Of course Mariah, regretted that she did that, but at that point it didn't matter to William. He wanted out of the marriage and used the fact that she compromised his business as a reason to do so. I thought what he did was lame. But hey, who am I? I'm just another woman scorned by her own ex-husband's indiscretions. But I'll tell you what; I won't be the only bitch around her crying much longer. Just wait and see.

Forty-five minutes had gone by and William was still a no show. I stood up and approached the receptionist again, "Would you see if William is still in that meeting?" I asked her.

"His hold calls light is still lit up so I'm afraid he's still unavailable. But you can certainly leave him a message and when he's done, I could have him call you." She told me.

"But I don't want a fucking phone call! What I've got to tell him doesn't need to be discussed over the damn phone." I snapped. This bitch was starting to get on my damn nerves.

"Ma'am I'm sorry but you're gonna have to lower your voice." She warned me.

"Or what?" I dared her.

"Or I'm gonna have to call security." She replied.

"Well, call 'em! I don't give a fuck!" I roared. By this time, I was angry. How dare she threaten me? Does she know who the fuck I am?

Without uttering another word, the receptionist picked up the phone and called for security. "Bill, will you have someone come up to the fifth floor? We have an irate woman yelling obscenities in the lobby area of the firm." I heard her say.

"Oh bitch! You haven't heard obscenities. Believe me, I've got more where that came from." I spat.

While I continued to scream on that dumb bitch, I realized that someone from security would be up here in the next minute or so to escort me off the premises and if I wanted to see William then I was going to have to take things into my own hands. So without giving that woman notice, I took off running down the hallway towards William's office. This place wasn't so big so I figured that his office couldn't be that far away. But to make things easier, I started yelling out his name. "William, where are you?" I yelled to the top of my voice. "I need to speak with you about Mariah." I continued.

Seconds later, William's head peered around the doorway at the far end of the hallway. "Kim is that you yelling like that?" He asked as he gradually walked out into the hallway to greet me.

"I came here to tell you that Mariah's dead. She committed suicide this morning at my home." I began to explain while I walked towards him.

"I already know." He replied. And before he could utter another word, both homicide detectives that were at my home to interview walked out of William's office and joined him in the hallway.

By the time I got within arms reach of William and the detectives, two security guards were down on my heels. They grabbed me by my arms and tried to pull me backwards. "Get the fuck off me!" I demanded, trying to break free of their grip.

"It's okay guys. Let her go." William instructed them.

Immediately after the guards released me, I stood my ground and snapped on their asses. "Touch me like that again and see what happens!" I warned them.

"Kim I'm gonna need you to calm down." William

said.

"I'm calm. I just didn't appreciate the way they grabbed me, so I had to address it." I told him.

"Do you need us to stick around Sir?" One of the guards asked William.

"No, you can go. I can handle it from here." William assured them. Then he turned his focus back on me. "Kim, I know you're upset about what Mariah did, but you can't come barging into my business with this type of behavior."

"So, that's it? That's all you've got to say about the mother of your children?" I commented. I was getting aggravated by the second while I waited for him to answer me.

"What else do you want me to say? She's gone. And she did it to herself." He continued.

"But she did it because you took away her fucking kids, you moron!" I snapped as I took two steps closer to him.

Both detectives probably figured that I was going to hit William because they stepped between us at that very moment. "All right! That's enough!" The male detective boomed, while the female detective grabbed my arm gently and pulled me in the opposite direction of William. That didn't stop me from cursing his insensitive ass out. "Yeah, get her ass out of here! She's an embarrassment." I heard him say.

"You're the fucking embarrassment! You fucking asshole!" I roared while I was still being led down the hallway.

"Don't ever let me see your face here again or I will have you arrested for trespassing." He warned me.

"That's all you know how to do is call the cops! Man up! You fucking pussy!" I blasted him before I was led around the corner. I thought the female cops was going to talk to me in the lobby area, but she escorted me onto the elevator and then she escorted me out of the building completely.

"You know if you come back here again, he can have you arrested, right?" She asked me.

"I don't give a damn about that!" I told her.

"Well, you should. Because it could very well happen."

"Well right now, getting arrested is the furthest thing from my mind. I just lost my best friend because of that idiot! And all he can say is that she did it to herself? How fucking pathetic can a person be? He's so self-absorbed is ridiculous."

"Look I know you're hurt behind your lost, and I'm sure you're right about him being pathetic, but you're gonna have to let him hang himself."

"Ughhhhh! I fucking hate him!" I screamed.

"Just calm down and take a deep breath. I know it doesn't seem like it, but things will get better." She commented while she rubbed my back in a circular motion.

"It sure as hell doesn't feel like it." I told her.

"Do you still have that card I gave you earlier this morning with the Chaplain's name and phone number on it?"

"Yeah, I got it. I left it on my coffee table at home." I replied.

"Well, give him a call. He's a great listener." She said and then stepped off and walked back into the building.

I stood there for a moment to collect my thoughts and that's when I realized that I didn't get the photos I needed to give to my enforcer. What the fuck was I thinking? I figured if I was going to hurry up and utilize my enforcer's special set of skills to eliminate that bastard, then I had to get to work. Hopefully Mariah has some recent photos of William. If not, then I'm screwed.

Back at Mariah's House

Thankfully I had a spare key to Mariah's house. I knew I'd have no distractions while I got through her things to find a photo of William's dumb ass. After I entered into the house, I dropped my handbag down on the loveseat by the front door and then I went straight into Mariah's hall closet where she kept her photo albums. She had a stack of them piled on top of one another so I took down the first three from the top. And what do you know, after opening the first photo album up, I run across a ton of photos of William while he was still married to Mariah. They were on their 5th wedding anniversary vacation in Turks & Caicos. Mariah looked so happy with this idiot, not knowing that this was going to be her last time celebrating their union.

Without giving it a second thought, I grabbed a photo that Mariah took of William by himself. I could tell that they had went on a fishing excursion while they were on vacation because in this picture William was standing on a boat holding a fishing rod in on one hand and a huge fish in another. He looked very proud of his catch. I'm sure Mariah felt otherwise. Mariah hated fishing. But she did it to appease that asshole of a man she used to have. She has always sacrificed things to make that Negro happy. And the crazy part about it is that he knew that about her. But instead of appreciating her, he continued to walk all over her and then out of the blue, then tells her he wants a fucking divorce. Now what type of bullshit is that? It's all good though, because I'm about to eliminate him altogether. I hope he's ready to go to hell.

I picked my handbag up from loveseat by the front door and stuck William's picture inside it. And while I was closing my handbag back up, I was startled by the sudden movement of the front door as it opened. My heart dropped into the pit of my stomach when Mariah's mother walked in immediately thereafter. "Oh my God! You scared me." I commented while I held my hand against my chest.

"What are you doing here?" she questioned me. I saw the pain in her face, so I knew she had been informed of Mariah's suicide.

Caught off guard by her question I thought for a second. I knew I couldn't tell her that I was there to find a picture of William so I could have him killed. So, what could I tell her? She walked closer to me, waiting for me to answer her. And then a thought came to me, "I came by to make sure everything in tact. You know, make sure all the windows and doors where locked." I finally said, even though every word I uttered was a lie.

She took a seat on the sofa and placed her purse on the coffee table. "Can you tell me exactly what happened to her?" She continued to question me. She gave me her undivided attention.

I sat down on the loveseat. I took a deep breath and then I exhaled. "Mrs. Elaine, I really don't know what to say." I said and then I paused.

"Just tell me what happened. I wanna know what made my daughter take her own life like that." Mrs. Elaine pressed the issue.

"All I know is that she called her divorce attorney bright and early this morning. But the conversation didn't go so well and Mariah got upset about it. I tried to calm her down but apparently it didn't work. So, while I was in the shower she went in my guest bedroom and hung herself from the coat rack in the walk-in closet."

"How long were you in the shower?" Mrs. Elaine asked, while started falling from her eyes. She seemed desperate for more answers.

"Give or take 15 to 20 minutes." I replied as I stood up from my seat and joined Mrs. Elaine on the sofa. I placed my hand on her back and started massaging it in a circular motion. "It's gonna be alright." I tried to comfort her.

"I just can't figure out why my baby would do that to herself. She was such a beautiful person and had so much to live for." She commented as she pulled a handkerchief from her purse. She immediately started wiping the tears away from her face.

"I know Mrs. Elaine. You're so right. I just wished she knew that." I agreed. Just thinking about the fact that I could've possibly saved her from committing suicide if I'd gotten out of the shower a few minutes sooner, filled me up with so much emotions and before I knew it, tears started falling rapidly from my eyes. Sitting here with Mrs. Elaine, I knew I wasn't going to be able to hang out with my best friend anymore. How could she do this to us? Did she not realize that her taking her own life would affect everyone that loved her?

Mrs. Elaine hung out at Mariah's place for the next hour or so. I helped her look for Mariah's life insurance information so we could contact the company and let them what was going on. I also helped her straighten up the house a little. When she noticed that one of the photo albums was open on the coffee table and a picture was take from the left side of the book, she questioned about it. "Was this photo album open like this when you got here?" She wanted to know.

"Yes it was," I lied.

Mrs. Elaine gave me a perplexed look. "I wonder why there's a missing picture from that page?" She wondered aloud.

"I wondered the same thing." I lied once again. Then I grabbed the photo album up from the coffee table and placed it back in the hallway closet where it belonged. Once Mrs. Elaine felt like Mariah's things were tidied up enough, she let me know that she was ready to leave. I joined her.

As soon as we walked outside, I walked Mrs. Elaine to her car. I promised her that I would check on her periodically. After I kissed her on her cheek, we said our goodbyes until the next time.

I watched Mrs. Elaine as she pulled away and thought to myself how strong of a woman she was. I also thought of the possibility that she may blame me for not saving her daughter's life when we were underneath the same roof. It would devastate me if I found out this was true. I know I wouldn't be able to deal with it.

Making A Trip To The Bank

As planned I made my way over to the bank so I could pull out $20,000 from my safe deposit box. Once I had it in hand, I stuck it deep down inside of my handbag and headed back out of the vault. On my way out of the bank I asked the bank manager for a large manila envelope. He reached behind his desk and pulled one from his drawers. "Is this large enough?" The white man asked me as he held it up to show me the size of it.

"Sure this is perfect. Thank you!" I said and took it from his hand.

I folded the manila envelope stuffed down inside of my purse and headed back out of the bank. While I was walking back to my car, I had this weird feeling come over me. It felt like someone was watching me. So, I carefully scanned my surroundings as I strolled back to where my car was parked. Thankfully I didn't see anyone lurking behind a bush or behind a pair of sunshades. If I had, I knew I would've freaked out.

Finally after driving for a total of 30 minutes, I made it back home. There was still yellow police tape wrapped around the trees and the entryway to my front door so I had to walk around my yard and take it all down. After I had taken it all down I disposed of it in the recycle bin alongside of my house. My neighbor Pamela Townson walked out onto her patio while I was making my way into my house. She stopped me in my tracks. "I'm sorry to hear about your friend." She said.

Pamela Townson was an older woman who was maybe in her late forties. She was an attractive woman. At first glance she resembled Vanessa Williams with the pretty eyes. She was married to a retired firefighter and he from what I hear he cheats on her just like everyone else's husband does. So, in retrospect, she doesn't have a life, which is why she's in everyone else's business.

"I appreciate that Pam. Thank you." I replied.

"If you need someone to talk to you know I'm here for you." She offered.

"I know you are. And thank you for that."

"Don't mention it." She said. Then she took a couple towards the edge of her patio. "Did your friend really hang herself from your walk-in closet?" She boldly asked me.

"No. It wasn't my bedroom closet. She hung herself in my guestroom walk-in closet." I explained.

"Oh wow! That's terrible. Are you going to be able to sleep in there by yourself, especially since this is so fresh?"

"I'll be all right."

"Well, if you need anything, just come and knock on the front door. You know my husband is never home so I could use the company." She said.

"I appreciate that. So, I'll definitely keep that in mind." I assured her and then I walked away. I couldn't get in my house quick enough for that nosey ass neighbor of mine. If I would've allowed her to question me for the next hour, the bitch would've done it. That's how lonely and bored she is with her life.

Inside my house, I dumped all of the money out of my purse and piled it on top of the kitchen table. I also grabbed the manila envelope and William's photo from my purse too. I smiled because I had everything my hit man needed to eliminate William's ass. It was just a matter of time before the job is executed.

Immediately after I stuffed the envelope with all of the goodies, I closed and sealed it up and then I held the package close to my heart. "See this right here is all I need to end that nigga's life. I literally had the keys to unlock the door to hell for him. And I can't wait to see the fruits of my labor."

I couldn't wait to get a taste of that sweet revenge. William will deserve everything he has coming to him. I just hoped that I get to witness it. I guess maybe I should put in that request the next time I speak to my hired muscle. Who knows, maybe he'd say yes. And even if he doesn't, then I'd still be cool with it. My

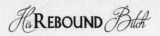

main objective is to get rid of all of these fucking cockroaches. They need to be off the streets once and for all. And I will make sure that it is done.

Making The Drop

Just like the hired hit man wanted, I drove out to the location and dropped the manila envelope in a mailbox at an abandon warehouse in the South Norfolk area of Berkeley. On my way back to my car, I sat there in the driver seat and dialed my hit man's number. He answered on the first ring. "I just dropped your gift off." I told him.

"I know." He said.

Caught off guard by his words, I scanned the area around me.

"It's okay. Don't be alarmed." He spoke into the phone.

"Where are you?" I asked him as I continued to look for him.

"That's not important." He replied nonchalantly.

"Oh okay." I said and drove away from the warehouse.

"The other thing is done." He uttered. "Go home and turn on the news." He said and then he disconnected our call.

I took my cell phone from my ear and placed it in the cup holder near the armrest. I can't lie I was spooked after I became aware that the hit man had watched me while I dropped off his package. While I drove back to my house I wondered if the hit man had initially followed me from the bank to my home. And if he had, had he watched my house and my movement up until this very moment. If that were true then when I had that weird feeling that someone was watching me while I was leaving the bank then I was probably right.

I rushed home because the hit man freaked me out and I needed to tune into to the news channel to get a full report on how my last victim was executed. It took me approximately 20 minutes to get back home. And as soon as I got out of my car, I raced inside of my home. I grabbed the remote control and powered on the TV. I quickly turned to the local news channel but when I got there, there was no new being reported. A Tide commercial was being played. Frustrated, I picked the remote back up and turned it to the next most popular news channel and BOOM, there it was. I immediately turned up the volume. "Virginia Beach police are baffled as to why a young woman that had just gotten off work was shot in the head execution style while she sat in her car in south entrance of the parking garage of the Town Center. A dozen of her co-workers and friends have congregated around the entrance of the parking garage mourning her death. Right now, the police say that they have no leads. But that they will pull the video footage from the cameras in the garage and interview as many people as they can so that they can find some answers. The identity of the victim won't be released until the family have been made aware of her death first. This is TV 12 news and I'm Brenda Wilcox reporting to you live in Virginia Beach." The reporter said.

I turned the volume back down on the TV and sat back on my living room sofa while I wrapped my brain around how my hit man murdered that home wreaking ass bitch! To hear the words execution style brought joy to my heart. I knew if people knew that I was behind these murders, they'd look at me like I was crazy or even call me an insane manic, but I to know that some of the women who had a hand in destroying my marriage and killing my unborn child, were no longer breathing made me feel vindicated. And I won't be satisfied until everyone has been eliminated.

The following morning I woke up at the crack of dawn. I headed towards the bathroom to take a shower but the energy from my guest room pulled me into that direction. I hadn't walked in that room since the cops left, so I was kind of afraid to go back in there and especially alone. But then I thought to myself, why be afraid? If Mariah's spirit was still lingering in there then it might be a good thing to see. So, after I turned the doorknob and pushed open the door, a small draft hit me in the face. The air was cool and it smelled fresh. So I inhaled it as I walked into the room. I sat down on the edge of the bed and stared into the walk-in closet where Mariah hung herself. I instantly became sad when I thought back on how her body fell onto the floor. I tried to hold my tears back but I couldn't. She killed herself in my house. She did it in this very room and it tears me up inside. "I'm going to make that bastard pay Mariah! I will not let him get away with what he did to you." I yelled as my words turned into cries. Mariah, if you can hear me right, just know that I love you and I got your letter. And I promise you that when I get your girls, I'm going to take care of them. You've got my word!" I continued to cry.

I sat there on the edge of the bed for at least another ten minutes and then I dragged myself into the bathroom and got in the shower. I stood there underneath the shower nozzle as the hot water penetrated my body. This was a sure way for me to calm down and relax. I eventually found peace within myself as I thought about the good times Mariah and I had. She was a great mother and a great friend. So I vow not to let her love for me and her children go unrewarded.

Messy Ass Bitches

ariah's mother called me around noon while I was on the hunt to check out my next victim. I was driving down Independence Boulevard when I answered her call. "Hi Kim, how are you?" She greeted me.

"I'm fine Mrs. Elaine. How are you?" I asked her.

"I'm not too good honey. I just got off the phone with William and he's giving me a hard time about seeing my grandkids."

"Why is that?" I asked. I was getting aggravated by the second.

"He said he hasn't told the girls about Mariah's death. And he wants to do that before he lets me see them." She explained.

"Why hasn't he told them yet?"

"He didn't say."

"Well did he tell you when you'd be able to see the girls?"

"All he told me was that he'd call me in a couple days."

"That's not right and he knows it. He's so freaking controlling it's pathetic." I spat.

"Do you think you could call him and maybe get him to change his mind?"

"Mrs. Elaine, William hates my guts. I doubt if he would even answer my call."

She sighed heavily. "I'm just gonna pray for him." She said.

"Yeah, do that. And pray for me while you're at it." I commented.

"All right baby, well I'm going to get off this phone. I've gotta call a few more of my relatives so they can help me arrange Mariah's funeral and wake."

"Mrs. Elaine, I already told you that I'd help you with that."

"I know you did baby. But, my family has already taken care of everything."

"Okay. Well if you need me for anything I'm only a phone call away."

"God bless you."

"God bless you too Mrs. Elaine." I replied.

Immediately after Mrs. Elaine disconnected our call, I sat there in the driver seat of my car and wondered to myself why did I say God bless you too? Did I really mean that? For whatever reason I said it and that's it.

My next victim's name was Fiona Lassiter. Just like everyone else she worked at my ex-husband's nightclub but she was a bartender. She only worked for him for about six months. She probably would've worked there longer if she hadn't gotten caught stealing money from the cash register. This bitch was on her grind. I mean, she literally fucked my husband's dick and fucked him out of thousands of dollars while she was making drinks.

Unfortunately for her silly ass, she works at another bar and I'm sure she makes far less than she did when she worked for my ex. She was a bartender for a sports bar near the oceanfront. So, I took a trip down to the spot to see her. She was there standing behind the bar when I walked into the place. I walked over and took a seat at the bar and asked her to make me a Whiskey Sour. She stood here and gave me a weird facial expression. "You look so familiar." She said.

"Are you from Texas?" I asked her, trying to throw her off.

"No."

"Well, that's where I'm from." I lied.

Fiona started making my drink but every other second or so, she'd look at me like she was desperately trying to figure out where she knew me from. I smiled at her the entire time. I loved playing this ridiculous game with her. Finally after she made my drink she placed it on the bar in front of me and tried to make out where she knew me from once more. "Did you ever work at a nightclub?"

"No. Never." I told her and then I took a sip of my drink.

"Awww man, this is killing me." She blurted out. "I hate it when I can't figure certain stuff out." She continued. I relished in the moment of having an upper hand in this situation. She was literally freaking out because she couldn't figure out how she knew me. Fiona was a very attractive young woman. She kind of put me in the mind of the actress Megan Goode. She had the same height and weight as the actress. Too bad, she didn't have Megan Goode's brains.

Fiona gave up on her guessing game and started helping a couple that strolled into the bar. I heard her giggling and chatting with them while she fixed their drinks. But what really caught my eye was when the woman got up and left her man at the bar while she made a bathroom run. Fiona didn't waste one minute to come on to the gentleman. He looked around the bar before he reached over the bar and grabbed her hand. "You better stop before she comes back." Fiona warned him in a playful manner. She was definitely a tease.

"Why don't you give me your number so I can call you later." He insisted.

"Are you going to make it worth my while?" She asked seductively.

"Oh most definitely." He told her and then he pulled his iPhone from the holster on his waist. "What's your number?" He continued as he keyed the numbers into his phone.

I swear I wanted to throw up all over the bar area. This bitch was a second class ho. If only the girlfriend of this man could see this bitch in action. To see this slick ass bitch get her ass kicked would be a treat.

After waiting for about five minutes, the girlfriend finally came back to the bar. She sat down beside her man and picked up their conversation where they left off. She even leaned over and kissed him in the mouth. Everything would've been cool that bitch Fiona would not have opened her mouth. "Awww, look at you two love birds! Y'all make such a good couple." She commented.

"Thank you." Both the woman and the man said.

I couldn't stand it any longer. This bitch was acting like she adored them. Really? I mean, she just gave the man her fucking cell phone number.

"What's your name sweetie?" I asked the girlfriend.

"Angela," she replied.

"Well Angela, this bitch behind the bar is fronting her ass off! She really could care less about how good you two look together because she just gave your man her cell phone number while you were in the bathroom."

The woman looked at Fiona and then she looked at her man. "Is this shit true?" she questioned him. Her pitch got a little high.

"I don't know what she's talking about." He replied nonchalantly.

Fiona stood there looking dumbfounded. But she stood her ground. "Me either. That's a lie! I didn't give him anything." She challenged me.

"Check his phone Angela. He just programmed it in there." I encouraged her.

"Give me your phone Paul. Let me see it now." She demanded.

Instead of handing over the phone, the guy stood up. He pulled money from his wallet for his drinks and dropped it on the bar. "I'm out of here." He said and walked away.

"Nigga you can leave all you want to but this shit ain't over. I'll deal with your ass in the car." Angela warned him.

Just like that, homeboy was out of there. Angela refused to leave though. She questioned Fiona again. This time she was standing on her feet. "Now bitch, I'm gonna only ask you once...." She began to say but Fiona cut her off in mid sentence.

"Bitch, you ain't gon' ask me shit! I already told you what time it was but if you wanna believe what she just said, then that's totally up to you." Fiona spat.

"Oh so now I'm a bitch?" Angela questioned her.

"That's how you're acting." Fiona replied.

And before I could blink one eye, Angela had jumped on top of the bar chair and hopped over the bar. She knocked Angela to the floor and started throwing blows to her face. "Who's the bitch now?" Angela roared as she pounced on Fiona.

"Get off of me. Somebody get her off of me." I heard Fiona screamed in shear pain.

I swear seeing this bitch get her ass kicked was truly epic. "Is someone going to break them up?" I heard a white woman from behind me ask while others looked on. There were only four other people in the bar area of this sports club and they were all glued to the commotion going on behind the bar counter.

I took the last sip of my cocktail, placed the glass down on the bar and left exactly $5 for my drink next to it. "Tootles!" I said and made my way out of the bar.

The guy that left his girlfriend in the bar was nowhere to be found when I walked into the parking lot to get to my car. I thought I'd see him sitting in his car, waiting for her to join him but he wasn't. I figured maybe he was driving his own car and decided to leave her there. Men! They are definitely selfish ass bastards!

While I was exiting the parking lot, two police squad cars made a beeline for the sports bar. It wasn't a mystery why they were going there. I knew after they were done investigating their altercation, both women would definitely be going to the nearest precinct. I kind of feel bad for the other woman because Fiona started that whole shit. Hopefully her cheating ass boyfriend gets her out of jail.

Dial 1-800-Missing

After that fiasco that took place at the sports bar I had to lay low for a couple of days. I hadn't heard from Mrs. Elaine nor had I heard a peep out of William. I searched every news channel to see if any more of my victims had met their fate, but so far nothing. So while I was lying in bed my doorbell rang a couple of times. I looked at the time to see the time and when I realized that it was a few minutes after ten, I scratched my head and wondered who it could be. I slipped on my night shoes and headed to the front door. I peered through the peephole and saw two black gentlemen standing on the other side of my front door. "Who is it?" I asked them.

It's Detective Bonds and Detective Green from Virginia Beach Police Department." One of the guys yelled.

I slightly cracked the door ajar. "How can I help you?" My questions continued.

The detective standing closer to the door spoke first, "Mind if we come in for a moment so we can speak with you about an altercation that happened two days ago at the sports bar on Independence Boulevard?"

"Was I in the fight?" I asked sarcastically.

"No ma'am you weren't. But we were told that you initiated it." The other detective spoke.

"I don't recall doing that officers." I told them.

"Ma'am we only have a few questions for you. So, the quicker you let us in, the faster we'll be out of your hair." The detective standing next to me chimed in.

"All right, but you better make this quick." I finally agreed and then I let both men into my house. "Have a seat on the sofa," I instructed them.

A few seconds after they both sat down, the detective who did the most talking at the front door pulled a photo from his jacket pocket. "Do you remember seeing this young lady at the bar?" He wanted to know.

"Not that I recall. Why?" I lied. I honestly didn't know what to say so the word no just spilled from my lips.

"Well because for one she was attacked by this woman here." He answered me and then he show me a photo of the chick Angela that was with her boyfriend at the bar the other day.

"Wow! That's not good." I commented.

"So, do you remember seeing this girl?" He continued to question me as he pointed to Angela's face.

"Well, she kind of looks more familiar to me than

the other girl." I lied once more.

"That sounds kind of strange coming from your mouth when we have the camera footage from the bar area of the sports bar and we have written testimonies from other bar patrons that puts you at the bar and at the heart of the altercation that took place."

"Oh really?" I replied casually. It didn't matter that they had me on camera and it didn't matter that they had other people to give them statements. I wasn't fighting so I couldn't care less about any of this.

"Listen Mrs. Weekes," the detective said.

"It's Ms. Weekes," I interjected.

"Ma'am the bartender went missing two nights ago and we were hoping that you could tell us anything about that day." The same detective said.

"Missing?" I replied surprisingly. A sharp pain shot through me. I felt a sense of nervousness. And then I started feeling hot around my armpits and the back of my neck. But I couldn't let them see me sweat.

"Yes, she went missing right after she was released from custody." The other detective spoke.

"Well, you need to be having his conversation with her family and not me." I replied cynically.

"Ms. Weekes, why did you start that argument between that bartender and the couple?" The same detective asked.

"I didn't start that argument." I snapped.

"Well, that's not what everyone there said."

"Do you think I care about what does people said?" I roared.

"Ms. Weekes, do you think the other woman had something to do with the bartender's disappearance?"

"I didn't know anyone of those women so I can't answer that. And if you don't mind, I'm gonna have to ask you two gentlemen to leave." I huffed and then I stood to my feet. I walked over to the front door and opened it.

"Well, we wanna thank you for your time." The other detective spoke.

"Don't mention it." I told him.

Immediately after they exited my home I closed the door and locked it. I rushed back over into my bedroom. I grabbed the remote from my bed and started sifting through channels. Once again I turned to the most popular news station but they was no news feed about Fiona. Then I turned it to the next news station and again, there was no news feed surrounding Fiona's disappearance. Were the detectives lying about Fiona being missing? Was this a trick of some sort? If so, then why?

Since I couldn't answer my own questions I picked up my cell phone and dialed my hit man's number. Like clockwork he answered on the first ring. "We need to talk." I told him.

"I'm gonna hang up and call you back." He replied and then the phone went silent.

Not even a second had passed and he called back. "What do you need?" He got straight to the point.

"I hear the girl's missing." I said, my voice barely audible. Thankfully he heard it.

"Yeah, she's gone. No one will ever find her." He assured me.

"What about the guy?"

"Just keep your television on the news channel." He insisted. "Anything else." He asked.

"No, that's it. Thanks." I said.

He didn't say another word. I knew he was gone because the phone line went silent again.

Who's Lurking In The Dark?

Later that night I finally decided to leave out of the house. I had a taste for some ice cream so I headed down to the 7-Eleven and picked myself up a pint of Ben & Jerry Strawberry Cheesecake ice cream. After I paid the cashier I took my ice cream and walked back out of the store. While I was getting back into my car, I had this weird feeling that someone was watching me, so I scanned the area around me. It was completely dark outside, so I really could see that far away but I looked anyway. And when I didn't see anyone looking in my direction, I got back into my car and drove away. Instead of going straight back to the house, I took a detour and decided to drive by Mariah's ex-husband's house. I was curious to see if that bastard was home.

It took me approximately 30 minutes to drive to his house. When I drove on his block, I noticed how peaceful it was. There was absolutely no one walking on these neighborhood streets. It was completely deserted. So, as I drove by William's house I cruised by it slowly so I wouldn't miss a thing.

Unfortunately, just like the streets I saw no movement inside the house. But I did notice that only

William's wife car was in the driveway. "It wouldn't surprise me if that nigga is out tonight cheating with the next chick." I mumbled underneath my breath. "And if he is, that serves his new wife right." I continued as I drove by.

I noticed there was only one light on in the house and that light was coming from the bedroom on the top floor. Judging from the windows, it looked like the master bedroom. So, I assumed that his wife was probably lying on the bed reading a book or something. I knew one thing, she better get used to being alone because after my hit man gets his hands on William, William will be pushing up daisies just like the rest of my victims on my shit list.

Seeing as though there wasn't any real action going on at William's house I kept driving up the block and found my way back to the highway. From there, I made my way back home.

Unexpected Call

My ex-husband called me out of the blue. When his cell phone number popped up on my caller ID, I was shocked considering I hadn't spoken to him in the last 6 to 8 months. "What do you want Drake?" I asked in an irritated fashion.

"I've got two questions." He replied.

I sighed heavily. "What is it?" The tone of my voice sounded even more irritated.

"I heard about Mariah so I wanted to call you and see how you were holding up."

"I was pretty shaken up about it when it first happened but I'm starting to come around. Thank you for asking." I said. I was shocked that this cheating ass nigga gave a damn about Mariah or myself. Was he starting to change his selfish ways?

"Have you spoken with William?"

"Yes, I talked to him and he acted like he could care less."

"That's not good."

"Tell me about it."

"So, how are her girls doing?"

"I don't think William has told them."

"Well he'd better hurry up because it's all over the news. And I knew he'd hate it if they found out while they were watching TV."

"Mariah's mom told him the same thing."

"Well then I hope he listens to her." Drake said and then he quickly went into the other reason why he called. "Are you spending anytime at our vacation home in the coming weeks?"

"No. Why?"

"Well, because I'm planning to go down there next weekend. And you know the judge said that we had to share the vacation home in Miami, so I wanted to give you advance just in case you were planning to go that same weekend."

"So, you're taking one of your new bitches down there, huh?"

"I wouldn't necessarily call anyone a bitch."

"I can't say mistresses because we're not married anymore." I commented.

Drake chuckled. "You're absolutely right." He replied and then he said, "Remember that young girl you accused me of cheating with?"

"There were tons of them, so which one are you talking about?"

"The one that worked at my night club. Her name was Sandy."

"Vaguely." I lied. "But what about her?" I continued.

"She just got arrested for killing her boyfriend."

"Oh pity her." I said unenthused. "Too bad she didn't kill you." I continued harshly. For one, I had already known about her arrest because I paid to have that bitch set up. And two, I really didn't care to talk about her. She got what she deserved. End of story.

"Why don't you just tell me to walk in front of a moving bus?" He nonchalantly.

"You know I would love to see that, right?" I replied sarcastically.

"Well that's too bad. It's not gonna happen." Drake said abruptly and then he said, "So, I guess this is when I say, have a nice day."

"Yeah, whatever." I responded and then we ended the call.

I sat there and thought about my talk with Drake. I've got to admit that he caught me off guard when he asked me about Sandy Pilar. I wasn't prepared to answer that question. Thankfully I was quick on my feet and didn't let on that I had already known what caused her arrest. I'm also thankful that he didn't mention anything about Melissa Carson being executed while she sat in her car in the parking garage. If he had, I can't say if I would've given myself away or what? I knew one thing though, I had to get myself

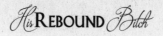

and my nerves under control before I sabotage my whole mission.

Lies On Top Of Lies

Mrs. Elaine waited three more days before she contacted me again. I was picking up some a few of my dresses from the dry cleaners. "How are you Mrs. Elaine?"

She let out a long sigh. "I'm doing okay I guess."

"Have you decided when Mariah's funeral is going to be?"

"Yes. It's gonna be this coming Saturday at 1pm at my church. And her wake will start tomorrow at Lovell's Funeral Home."

"What time will the funeral home have her ready so we can view her body?"

"They said that family and friends could start coming by anytime after 12 noon."

"And what's the name of the church you belong to?"

"The Church of Christ on Providence Road."

"Is it going to be open or close casket?"

"Open."

"What about the girls? Are they coming?"

"Yes, William finally told them yesterday. So, he's going to meet the family at the church around 12:30."

"Has he mentioned anything about you spending time with the girls now that Mariah is gone?"

"Well, I asked him if they could stay with me for a couple of days after the funeral but he hasn't given me an answer as of yet."

I could tell that Mrs. Elaine was really broken up about her grandkids. It was bad enough that she had just lost her only child so to be unable to see and spend time with her daughter's children is just down right hateful.

"Mrs. Elaine, all you can do is pray for him. God will handle him." I told her. But in the back of my mind, I really didn't feel that way. I knew God could handle every situation we brought to Him. And I also knew that God wouldn't help me commit murder. So I took things into my own hand and paid a hit man to take revenge on all the women that caused me all my heartache and pain. I figured my way was the best way.

"You said a mouthful when you brought God into this conversation. God will definitely handle William. And He's going to soften William's heart so that I can spend time with my grandkids. Wait and see."

"Oh I believe it." I told her. "Now if you need anything before I see you at the funeral just give me a call, okay."

"I will baby. Now you keep your head up."

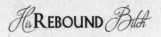

"I will Mrs. Elaine and thank you." I said.

After I got off the phone with Mrs. Elaine I decided to take a drive by William's house again. I figured since the weather was beautiful outside there would be a chance that I'd see the girls playing in the front yard.

During the drive to William's house had me on high alert. William was a self-employed man. So that meant he could leave his office anytime he felt like it. Instead of taking my normal route I took the back roads. And when I arrived in his neighborhood, I took the back streets and drove by his block just to make sure his car wasn't in the driveway and when I noticed that it wasn't I exhaled. I turned my car around and made the turn on his street because I needed a closer look. Once again I found the street to be quiet like the other night. But as quickly as I exhaled and offered compliments about how peaceful the block was, I was startled by sudden movement to the right of me. I tried to use my peripheral vision but my head wasn't in the right position to do so. So I turned my head slightly to the right and that's when I saw William's wife Tammy sitting in her car parked across from her house. She looked like she was looking down at something. But that only lasted seconds because our eyes met. I swear I didn't know if I should speed off or stop to say hi. I did know that if I didn't stop, she'd have a lot to tell her husband the next time she talked to him.

Without giving it a lot of thought, I stopped my car directly beside hers and rolled down my passenger side window. "Hi Tammy, how are you?" I greeted her with the fakest smiled I could muster up.

It was kind of awkward but she smiled back. "I'm doing okay. And you?" She replied.

"I'm okay I guess." I told her. "So what are you doing parked on this side of the street?" I asked her.

"William and I had our landscapers come out to spray our lawn with the True Green Formula so I parked my car on this side of the street so that now of the chemicals wouldn't get on my car."

"Oh well that was smart." I commented. "So, is William home?" I asked.

"No. He left for work early this morning."

"Well, I'm sure you heard what happened to Mariah?" I continued.

"Yes, I did." She said in an apologetic manner. "When William told me what happened I felt so bad for her. And I really feel bad for the girls too because now they're not gonna have their mother in their lives anymore."

"How did the girls take it when William told them?"

"He hasn't told them yet. He's trying to find a good time to find a good time to break the news to them."

"But I thought he had already told them." I replied in an irritated manner. He knew he was wrong for lying to Mrs. Elaine.

"No. He hasn't."

"Well he'd better do it soon because the funeral is the day after tomorrow."

"Yeah, I know. Mrs. Elaine called and told us."

"Does he plan to let Mrs. Elaine spend time with the girls after the funeral?"

"He hasn't mentioned anything to me about it so I'm not sure." She replied. But I knew the bitch was lying. Mariah told me how this bitch was. Tammy knew everything that went on between William and Mariah, especially if it had something to do with the girls. At that very moment, I wanted to hop out my car and drag that bitch up and down this street for starting all that shit that happened a week ago and caused Mariah to get arrested. It could've been avoided. But no, this bitch here wanted to show her ass while William was by her side. And now that she's alone, she wants to play like she's a sweetheart and that she's concerned about Mariah and the girls. But bitch please! I can see through all your bullshit.

"Listen Tammy, I want to believe that you have a good heart. So, if you do, please talk to William and convince him to let those girls spend a few days with their grandmother. That would mean the world to her. Now can you do that?" I asked her. Once again, I tried to put on the fakest smile I could muster up.

"You know how stubborn William is so I will try." She replied.

"Okay." I said. "Have a nice day." I continued and then I rolled my passenger side window back up. I drove away from that conversation pissed off. The nerve of that bitch! She and William will definitely get what's coming to them. Mark my words!

To Kill Or Be Killed

The funeral home was dark and gloomy looking on the inside. I was greeted by one of the funeral home representatives when I walked through the front door. I was also told to sign in before I went inside the chapel area to view Mariah's body. The air was cold. I figured it was this way because the room was empty. So as I walked towards Mariah's casket I felt a cloud loom over me. I was only a few feet away from her and I could see that she that she looked like she was at peace. So I walked closer. And when I was finally within inches of her I was able to take everything in. Mariah didn't look like herself but I knew it was her. Her skin was darker and her face was much larger. Had the funeral home officials embalm her with too much embalming fluid? And why did she have on so much make-up? Mariah hated make-up. All she ever wore was lip liner and lip-gloss. So to see my best friend like this didn't sit well with me. Who dropped the ball on this?

While I stood there grieving because of how my best friend was being sent away, feelings of how she was being bullied started boiling inside of me. I knew she wouldn't even be in this fucking casket right now if she was being created fairly. Mariah was a loving mother, daughter and a friend. She didn't have a mean bone in her entire body so take her through unnecessary bullshit? "Don't worry Mariah, I promise I am going to make sure he pays for this." I said, my words were barely audible because of my constant crying.

"She looks peaceful doesn't she?" A voice asked me. Whoever it was, was standing behind me. Startled by the sudden presence of someone else, I turned around. "When did you two come in here?" I asked the Homicide Detectives that interviewed me after Mariah committed suicide. The male detective to the side while the female carried on the conversation with me.

"We just got here like one minute ago." She told me. "And I was saying that she looked peaceful." She continued.

Thrown completely off my square, I turned away from the female detective and looked back at Mariah. My mind was running at a fast pace. I didn't know whether to agree with the cop or try to figure out if she heard me when I promised Mariah that I was going to make sure William paid for her death. Everything was all a big blur to me. "Yeah, she does look peaceful." I finally agreed. Then I turned my focus back to the cop. "I really appreciate you two coming down here to pay your respects to Mariah." I continued, trying to look less awkward.

"No problem.   But that's why we're here." She replied.

"I don't follow you." I mentioned, trying to figure out what she wanted.

"Well, Detective Logan and I are investigating an execution style murder that happened in the parking garage of Town Center the other day.   And after compiling all of the surveillance footage taken that day from the parking garage, the streets cams and the security cameras from the restaurant the victim stopped by for lunch with a co-worker, we found you in a lot of the frames.   So, can you tell us what you were doing that day while you where in Town Center?" Detective Bower said.

The temperature around my neck and underneath my armpits became hotter.   Plus my mind started racing at an uncontrollable speed.   I didn't know if I was coming or going.   I also didn't know what the fuck to say.   Shit, I couldn't tell her I was there spying on that bitch.   I wasn't giving myself away.   No way.

"All I remember doing is parking my car in the garage, then I stopped by the coffee shop and then I decided to go over to the restaurant so I could get me a cocktail." I finally explained.

"Did you know this young lady?" The female detective asked me as she whipped out a photo of

Melissa Carson.

I pretended to look at Melissa's photo long and hard. "Not that I recall." I lied.

"Are you sure?" Detective Bower pressed the issue.

"Yes, I'm sure." I assured her.

"Do you remember seeing anyone inside of the restaurant or in the parking garage that looked suspicious?"

"No. Not that I recall." I told her.

"Okay. Well, take my care," she said and handed it to me. "If something comes to you after we leave, please don't hesitate to call me."

I took the card from her hand and placed it inside of my handbag. "I will." I replied.

"Thanks for your time." The female detective said.

"Don't mention it." I told her and then I watched her as she and her male partner leave the funeral home.

After I watched her walk out of the door of the funeral home I almost collapsed right here on the fucking floor. I mean, did she just come in here and ask if I knew Melissa Carson? The bitch that used to be one of my husband's mistresses. And did she just ask me if I remember seeing anyone that looked suspicious while I was in the parking garage and the restaurant? Did she really think that I was going to do her work for her? Fuck no! I was on a mission to eliminate everyone on my list and if she thinks that

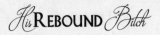

she's going to come between that, then I guess that she
would be next.

Ashes To Ashes — Dust to Dust

Today was the day that my best friend's only living parent was sending her home to be with God. It was a very sad occasion. Mrs. Elaine's small church was filled to capacity. I didn't know Mariah's family was so big. I walked into the church and took a seat in the third row. I shook a few people's hands while I introduced myself. William came strolling in with his wife Tammy and the girls. I was so happy to see those little ladies. He and his wife Tammy took a seat on the second row with other family members, while the girls sat on the first row with their grandmother Mrs. Elaine.

Shortly thereafter, the service started. One of Mariah's cousins sung a beautiful song, while a couple of the neighbors shared a few memorable encounters they had with Elaine. In all, the service was nice.

Immediately after the service everyone followed the hearse to the burial sight. I was surprised to see William and Tammy attend that part of the funeral. But he did. The girls were taking it really hard knowing that their mother was going to be gone away from them forever. While they stood there in front of the casket, I wanted to walk over and comfort them so badly, but I knew William wouldn't have it. Knowing how ignorant he was, he'd probably try to snatch them from my grasp.

After the final prayer everyone depart ways and headed to their cars. William grabbed both of the girls' hands and headed in the direction of his car while Tammy followed. I rushed over to Mrs. Elaine who was talking to a family member. "Excuse me," I said looking at Mrs. Elaine and the other woman and man that was before her. "Did William ever say whether he was going to let the girls spend time with you after the funeral?" I continued.

"No, he never said anything else about it." Mrs. Elaine replied.

"Well, he's got the girls and they're about to get in his car and leave." I rushed to say.

"Would somebody go and tell him that I need to speak with him before he leaves?" Mrs. Elaine asked.

"I'll do it." I volunteered and then I rushed off towards the direction William parked his car. "Hey William, wait." I yelled halfway towards him.

He turned around and stood still while Tammy kept walking with the girls. I was winded when I got within arms reach of him. I tried to catch my breath. "Hey William, Mrs. Elaine said she needs to speak with you before you leave." I belted it out between breaths.

"Tell her I'll give her a call later." He replied nonchalantly and then he turned around to walk off.

"But she's only a few feet away from us." I argued.

"And I have somewhere to be." I said while he continued to head towards his car.

"Come on William, you know she wants to spend a few days with the girls so why don't you just allow her to do that?" I pressed the issue.

"Tell her to come by my house and she can spend time with them there." He told me and then he got into his car.

"You are such a fucking dickhead!" I yelled at him as he closed the driver side door closed.

I thought he was going to respond to my rude outburst but he didn't. Instead, he sped off into the sunset. I swear, I had so many other things I wanted to say to him but time wasn't on my side. But I will have the last laugh.

I didn't have to tell Mrs. Elaine what William said, she saw his body language when I was talking to him, so she was able to read between the lines. To cheer her up, I did tell her that he offered to have her over to his house so she could visit the girls. She became excited about that. "So, what are you going to do now?" I asked her.

"All of my family members are going to go back to my house for the repass and talk about how good the Lord is." She smiled.

"Sounds like a plan." I commented.

"Amen!" She replied and then she winked her eye at me.

I promised I would come by her house later after I went home to change into some comfortable clothes. "You better." She said and then we parted ways.

Public Enemy #1

Seeing the cops the yesterday at the funeral home spooked the hell out of me. Were they on to me? Did they know more than what they were telling me? Whatever they knew, they'd better use it because I'd never give myself up. Not now. Not ever.

I rushed home and changed into something more comfortable, since I knew I would be hanging out at Mrs. Elaine's house for a couple of hours. So after I slipped on some casual attire I jumped back into my car and headed over to her house.

Cars flooded Mrs. Elaine's street. It was truly hard to find a parking space but somehow I managed. One of Mariah's cousins opened the door and let me in the house. I did my round and spoke to everyone I knew and then I eased my to the back of the house were Mrs. Elaine was. She was sitting on the back patio with some other elderly women. I spoke to everyone and then I took a seat by Mrs. Elaine. She patted me on my back. "I'm glad you came back." She said.

"I wasn't going to stand you up like that." I told her.

"Can y'all give me and her a few minutes alone?" She asked the other three women who were all sitting in a huddle.

"Sure. No problem." They said in unison and then they got up and left.

"Did you eat?"

"No. But I'll get some later." I replied. "I'm more interested in you right now." I continued.

"You know he hasn't called and said anything to me about seeing my grandbabies."

"That's because he's a jerk. He knows what those girls mean to you."

"It's okay. The Lord is going to take care of him."

"Have you tried to call him since he left the grave sight?"

"No. I figured if he wanted to talk to me then he'd call me."

"And I truly agree." I chimed in. "You know you may have to go the court

to request visitation rights?" I asked her.

"I've thought about that."

"Well, if you want me to help you, then I'll take you down there whenever you're ready."

"I appreciate that darling." She replied and then she robbed my back in a circular motion.

"Mrs. Elaine do you blame me for Mariah's death?"

"Oh no baby! Why would you say that?"

"Because I was in the house with her. I was only ten feet away from her and if I hadn't been in the bathroom for so long then I could've saved her life."

"Well, you can get that nonsense out of your head because that thought never crossed my mind. I appreciate the friendship you had with my baby Mariah. She loved you like a sister. So, for that I will always look at you as my child."

"Thank you Mrs. Elaine."

"Don't mention it." She said. "Well, let me get back in this house. I've gotta sit in a more comfortable chair." She continued as she stood to her feet.

"Come on, let me help you." I insisted while I helped her stand to her feet. A few seconds later, I led her into the house.

I hung around Mrs. Elaine's house for a couple of hours and then I decided it was time to leave. I kissed her on her cheeks and said goodbye before I made my exit. While I was walking to my car I couldn't help but think how sad Mrs. Elaine was behind Mariah's death and the fact that William wouldn't let her see her grandkids. But then I reminded myself that this to shall pass. After my hit man finished William's punk ass off, then Mrs. Elaine would be able to have her grandkids in her care for good. It can't get any sweeter than that.

Your Time Is Up

O n my way home I couldn't get that bastard William out of my head. The way he played Mrs. Elaine wasn't cool. I couldn't wait until my hit man ended his life. He didn't deserve to live anymore, especially after causing my best friend's death. No way. He had to go.

At the last minute I decided to drive by his house. I wanted to have a face to face with him because this shit was getting out of hand. "We're going to handle this situation once and for all." I mumbled to myself.

Normally it would only take me 20 minutes to get to William's house, but for some reason I got there in 15 minutes. It was a few minutes after 8:00 pm. so it was dusk outside. When I pulled up in front of William's house I noticed that his car wasn't parked alongside of his wife's Tammy's car. I even noticed that there were no lights on in the house so I knew instantly that no one was there, which was why I didn't knock on their front door.

I knew William like the back of my hand. He wasn't the stay out late kind of guy. I knew he'd be home very soon, which was why I decided to sit in my car and wait for their arrival. I popped in a K. Michelle CD and allowed this music to occupy my time while I waited for this asshole to get here.

Three songs played before I finally saw a set of headlights in my rearview mirror. I knew the headlights on the car belonged to William so I sat up in the seat and started rehearsing in my head how I was going to talk to William about the girls. The car drove by my car slowly and as it passed me I turned to look and Tammy's eyes locked with mine. I saw her mouthing something. I couldn't quite figure out what she was saying but I knew it was about me and it wasn't nice.

Immediately after William parked his car beside Tammy's car I rushed out of my car so that I could meet him as soon as he got out of his car. Tammy and the kids got out first. "Hi girls," I waved.

"Hi Ms. Kim," they both replied in unison.

"Hi babies. You two looked so beautiful today." I complimented them while Tammy walked ahead of them. I totally ignored her ass.

"Are you coming over here to get us?" One of the girls asked, while they both stood next to their dad's car.

My heart melted that instant. I could see it in their eyes that they wanted to leave this Godforsaken house. "No, she's not here to pick you girls up. Now go in the

house with Tammy and I'll be there in a minute."
William interjected.

"William why won't you let me take them to see
their grandmother?" I asked as I turned my attention to
him.

"What do you want?" He asked me. It was evident
that he wasn't going to answer my question.

"I came over here to see if you'd change your mind
about letting Mrs. Elaine spending time with the girls.
You see they wanna come with me."

"Well, that's too bad because they're not going."
He replied and then he started walking up the driveway
towards the front door.

"Why not?"

He stopped in his tracks and abruptly turned
around. "Do you think I'm going to let my daughters
be somewhere where they are constantly reminded
about their mother's death? Do you think that would
be healthy for them?" He asked sarcastically.

"Them spending time with their grandmother is the
healthiest thing you could do for them right now."

"Well it's not gonna happen now get off my
property and don't ever bring your ass back over here!"
He spat and stormed off in the direction of his house.

"You're a fucking asshole! You know that?" I
roared.

"Fuck you bitch! Now if I gotta tell you to get off

my property again, I'm gonna have your ass arrested!"
He threatened and then he went inside of his house and
slammed the front door.

Instead of standing there in his driveway, I headed
back to my car. I refused to give him the pleasure of
calling the cops on me. He'd love seeing me get put in
handcuffs. He's a miserable ass nigga! And I can't
wait until his ass gets dealt with. In my mind, William
was overdue for a wake-up call. So, it was time to get
my hit man on the line. I needed to know why this
nigga hadn't gotten dealt with yet.

Right after I got into my car, I pulled out my cell
phone and immediately started dialing my hit man's
number. Like always he answered on the first ring.
"Yes," he said.

"When are you taking care of my new problem? I
can't go another day like this." I blurted out knowing
that I knew this guy didn't like to talk about his hits
until he calls me back on his unsecured line. But I
didn't care. I needed an answer now.

"I'm taking care of it now." He said.

Shocked by his answer, I asked him to repeat
himself. "What did you just say?"

"Look up and turn your head to the right," he
instructed me. Just as he instructed me to do, I looked
up and turned my attention to the right of me. I
couldn't see anything in the darkness besides William's

house. I blinked and squinted my eyes to readjust them. "What am I supposed to be looking at?" I asked him. I was becoming frustrated. Then out of the darkness I saw a flicker of light. That flicker of light came from the screen of the hit man's cell phone when he took it away from his ear. My heart sunk in the pit of my stomach when he illuminated his face with the light from his cell phone. And as quickly as I saw his face, that's how quickly, it disappeared. "Hello," I said.

"Get out of here," he said and then the line went dead.

Anxiety filled my entire body. I knew that William was about to get what the fuck he deserved. And finally Mariah will get her dying wish. "Kill that son of a bitch!" I said, gritting my teeth and then I smiled as sped off into the night air.

A Mistake Has Been Made

I tossed and turned all night. I couldn't sleep one wink. I kept the TV on just in case a news broadcast alert popped up. I knew I couldn't call my hit man to get the details about how he killed William, so I began to get a heavy case of anxiety. I started to jump in my car and ride by William's house to see if the cops were there, but then I decided against it. I knew that would be a very bad idea. The cops had already questioned me once; I'd be stupid if I got caught riding around in that neighborhood. So, I did the next best thing, and that was stay glued to the TV in my bedroom.

I hopped out of bed and grabbed myself a cup of hot tea from the kitchen. A few minutes later I climbed back into my bed, grabbed the remote control and started flipping back and forth though the local news station channels. There was absolutely nothing going on so I looked at my alarm clock and noticed that only thirty minutes had passed. I was going out of my mind while the time crept by. "Ugh! What the fuck is taking so long?" I said in hast. Time was definitely not working in my favor. I wanted answers now. I was ready to pat myself on the back for the good deed I did for my best friend Mariah. I wanted to feel like I'd accomplished something. But for some untimely reason, that wasn't happening.

I couldn't take it anymore. I sat my coffee mug down next to the lamp on my end table and jumped to my feet. "Fuck this! I refuse to sit around here any longer." I huffed.

After grabbing a sweatshirt, a pair of sweat pants and socks from my dresser drawer, I got dressed pretty quickly. Then I slipped on a pair of my running sneakers. I raced towards the living room with my cell phone in hand so I could grab my car keys from the table by the front door but I was stopped in my tracks when my cell phone started vibrating in my hand. I looked down at the caller I.D. and saw that Mariah's mother was calling me. I pressed the SEND button. "Hello," I said.

"Kim, William has been shot and now the paramedics are on their way to the emergency room. So, I'm heading to the hospital. Tammy and the kids are going to meet me there." Mrs. Elaine said frantically.

"What do you mean he was shot? Who shot him?" I tried to probe her for answers.

"I don't know."

"Is he dead?" I pressed her. I needed to know if he was dead or not.

"I don't know."

"Is Tammy and the girls alright?" My questions continued.

"Yes, they're fine. Just meet me at the hospital now." She said and then she ended our call.

Anxiety filled my entire body as I replayed the events that happened tonight leading up to William getting shot by my hit man. God I prayed that that monster was either dead or dying. I couldn't have him around anymore. He was causing too much trouble. I can't wait to celebrate his demise in secret. Revenge was the best weapon for people like my best friend Mariah and I. The moment you cause us heartache, that's the moment you seal your fate.

The drive to the hospital only took me fifteen minutes. Immediately after I rushed inside of the emergency area waiting room I saw Mrs. Elaine holding one of the girls while Tammy held onto Mariah's other daughter. I took a seat next to Mrs. Elaine. She rubbed my knee. "I really appreciate you coming down here like this." She thanked me.

"Don't mention it." I replied and then I kissed her on the right side of her cheek. "Any word yet on William's condition?" I went into question mode.

"No, not yet. And they're taking so freaking long to send someone out here to tell us what's going on." Tammy answered first.

"What exactly happened?" I asked her. I needed some details and I needed them quickly.

"Right now isn't the time to talk about this around the kids." Mrs. Elaine interjected.

Frustrated by everyone's tight lips I sighed loud enough for only I could hear it. I mean, what was I supposed to do? Just sit here in limbo and wait for somebody to fucking talk about what happened? This shit was becoming unbearable by the fucking second.

Since no one was talking I pulled out my cell phone and logged onto the local news website to see if anyone was talking about the shooting. While I strolled through the pages of the site I heard footsteps coming in our direction. I looked up from my cell phone and there standing before us was Detective Bonds and Detective Green from Virginia Beach Police Department. I swear I wanted to die right then and there. "Mrs. Weekes, it's weird seeing you here." Detective Bonds spoke first.

"I'm only here to comfort my late best friend's mother and children." I replied, giving them both eye contact.

"Well, excuse us while we speak with Mrs. Slone privately." The same detective said and turned his attention towards Tammy.

Tammy passed Mariah's other daughter off to me and then she followed both detectives to the other side of the emergency waiting room. I couldn't hear what they were saying, so I watched Tammy's body movement while she answered their questions.

I looked down at the girls and noticed that they were both asleep while they lied on our laps. I figured now would be a good time to get a few answers out of Mrs. Elaine. "I hope he pulls through this." I said to Mrs. Elaine, hoping she fall for the bait.

She looked at me and then she looked down at both of the girls. After she saw that their eyes were closed, she broke her silence. "As much as I dislike him, I hope he pulls through too. I mean, especially for the girls'. It would be devastating for them to lose their mother and then lose their father not even a week later." Mrs. Elaine pointed out.

"Yes, that would be devastating." I agreed in front of Mrs. Elaine. But on the inside I was cringing at the idea of that bastard living through this ordeal. His time here on earth has run out and I had to make sure of that.

"I sure hope those cops find out who that guy was and give him the death penalty."

"Did they get a look at him?" My questions began as my heart rate picked up. I knew deep in my heart that Tammy told Mrs. Elaine something.

"No. Tammy said the guy was wearing a ski mask."

"Where was she? And how did she see him?"

"She said that she was upstairs in the bed while William was downstairs working in his home office. Then all of a sudden she heard some noise coming from his office so she jumped up."

"What kind of noise?" I asked.

"She said it sounded like William had fallen and hit the floor. So, she called his name and when he didn't answer she got up from the bed and rush downstairs. And that's when saw a guy with a black, ski mask bailing out of the back door to their house. She said she yelled and screamed to the top of her voice hoping one of the neighbors would hear her. Meanwhile she saw William lying on the floor of his office bleeding from his chest so she called 911."

"Wow! I knew that was very traumatic for her."

"Of course it was. Seeing your husband dying right before your eyes and you can't do anything about it. I'm just surprised at how she's keeping it together." Mrs. Elaine said as she looked over at Tammy, while she was still talking to the detectives.

"I wonder what they're saying to her." I commented immediately after I turned my attention towards Tammy and the cops.

"Probably route stuff," Mrs. Elaine guessed.

I sat there and wondered what the detectives and Tammy were talking about. I got to admit that I was a fucking nervous wreck. I knew that those cops couldn't link me directly to this shooting but I figured if they dug in deep enough and found any forensics that would lead them to my hit man, then there was a strong possibility that the hit man could rat my ass out. So, right now I needed one of those doctors to come out here and tell me that that bastard William is dead. Nothing else would put me at peace.

Someone Dropped the Ball

The detectives talked to Tammy for at least thirty minutes or so. I swear I don't know I was able to keep my composure. It seemed like every other time when the cops would ask her a question she would look back at Mrs. Elaine and I before she answered it. That shit was becoming nerve wrecking. Thankfully all of that came to halt when an Asian doctor walked into the waiting room and called Tammy's name. "I'm right here." She made herself known.

Mrs. Elaine and I both stood up and met Tammy and the doctor in the middle of the floor. "Mrs. Slone, your husband is in a coma." He started off. Tammy stood there motionless. She wouldn't utter one word. So, Mrs. Elaine talked for her.

"What does that mean? Will he come out of it?"

"Whoever shot him obviously wanted him dead. Mr. Slone suffered two gun shot wounds to the chest. He has lost a tremendous amount of blood and it looks like he may not even make it." He explained.

Tammy fell to the floor on her knees. "Noooooo! Please try to do everything you can. I can't live without my husband!" She cried out.

The Asian doctor reached down and tried to console Tammy. He pulled her back up from the floor. "What are the odds of him pulling through?" I asked.

"The odds are very slim. Right now, we have him in an induced coma because the two rounds traversed his chest from the front to the back and generated an extremely destructive cavitation shockwave that obliterated most of the tissue within a radius several inches from the trajectory. Then as the bullet traveled it struck the spinal column at an angle making an instant exit out of his back. So upon exiting the back the rounds made the exit wounds many times larger than its original (bullet-sized) entry point. And because of the loss of all consciousness has caused an abysmal loss of blood pressure to the brain, which will cause irreversible brain damage." The doctor continued to explain.

"So what is this? A waiting game." I interjected.

"Pretty much." The doctor replied.

"So, there's nothing you can do to save my husband?" Tammy chimed in as the tears fell down her face. She looked so out of it.

I saw the detectives looking at Mrs. Elaine, Tammy and myself through my peripheral vision while we huddled around the doctor. I knew that they were studying our body language.

"Not really. All we can do now is hope for a miracle." He replied.

"So, when can we see him?" Tammy wanted to know.

"Give them nurse a few minutes to set him up in the I.C.U. When they're done then they'll call you." He assured us.

"Thank you doctor." I said, acting like I was sincerely concerned. I had to fake it for the cops who weren't budging. They were literally watching us like a fucking hawk.

After the doctor walked away I made my way back over to where we were sitting before the doctor came out with the news. Mrs. Elaine followed me. The detectives asked Tammy if they could bother her for a few more minutes. She said yes and headed back to where they were standing.

"Think Tammy will pull the plug on William?" I immediately went back into question mode.

"She may not have a choice. The doctor said that the chances for William pulling through are nearly impossible." Mrs. Elaine replied.

Instead of responding to Mrs. Elaine's statement, I went into silent mode. My mind starting running at full speed and the what if's began to plague me. I needed for William to die right now. I also needed for the detectives to stop asking questions too. This thing has got to go away immediately. I won't be able to move forward unless it does.

The detectives talked to Tammy for another ten minutes or so and then they left. About thirty minutes or so after that, the nurse from ICU came out and escorted Tammy, Mrs. Elaine, the girls and myself back to William's room. When I entered the room I felt a cold draft immerse my entire body. I felt out of place. I knew I shouldn't be here. I wanted this man dead. He doesn't deserve to live, especially after the way he treated my best friend.

Mrs. Elaine and I took a seat and placed the girls on our lap while Tammy stood by William's bedside. I watched her as she rubbed his arm and stroked her fingers through his fine curly hair. "William, please come back to us baby. The girls and I need you here." She began to sob quietly.

I sat there and watched how Tammy tried to comfort William by rearranging his bed sheets and the life support tubes and monitor instruments that were connected to him. She kissed him over a dozen times. She even expressed her love to him as if he could respond. From that moment, I could see the love she had for this man. William was a piece of shit but to her, he was the apple of her eye. She found no fault in him, while the rest of us hated his fucking guts.

It seemed like every other second the nurses were in the room doing something to William. It became a circle at one point so I threw up my hands and excused myself. I kissed both of the girls and told Mrs. Elaine I'd check on her later. On my way out of the hospital room, I hugged her and told her I'd be praying for her and William. She gave me a half smile and thanked me for coming by.

While I headed towards my car I saw the sun coming up. The sunrise was beautiful but I couldn't appreciate the beauty of it because of the major dilemma back in the hospital. I can't believe how my hit man dropped the fucking ball on this hit. William wasn't supposed to be alive when I walked into ICU. What if he wakes up? He could fuck things up for me. I know one thing my hit man had some explaining to do. I paid for a dead man, not a fucking man lying in a coma.

Immediately after I got inside of my car, I sped into the direction of my apartment. In route to my place, I stopped by Mc. Donald's drive thru for a hot cup of coffee. After the cashier handed me my drink I pulled off and parked my car in an empty space of the fast food's chain parking lot. I grabbed my cell phone from my handbag and dialed my hit man's number. He answered on the first ring. "What can I help you with?" he spoke first.

"We need to talk now." I replied in an alarming manner. I was fucking furious and the tone of my voice made it very clear.

"I'll call you back on a secured line." He told me and then he disconnected our call.

I took a sip of my coffee and waited for him to ring my cell phone back. Several seconds later, it happened. I answered his call on the first ring. "What happened? Why is he still alive?" I roared into the phone.

"He won't be for long." The hit man spoke calmly but in a demonic kind of fashion.

"How do you expect that to happen?" I asked sarcastically.

"I'm not at liberty to say. But I will tell you that it will be done soon." He continued, the tone of his voice didn't change.

"That's not good enough! I paid for you to execute this hit and you dropped the ball. Do you realize that that bastard could wake up at any given moment?" My voice boomed. The hit man needed to know that this situation was serious. I paid good money for William to be in a body bag. So for me not to get my money's worth, rubbed me the wrong way.

"I told you that I am going to handle it. Now let me do my job." He told me and then without any warning, he disconnected our call.

I sat there in my and huffed in frustrations. How the hell did you fuck that job up? This guy was supposed to be the best. So, why did he screw this shit up? I can tell you right now that the cops are going to be swarming that hospital. And if my guy thinks that he's going to get passed them, then he's got another thing coming.

As soon as I walked into my apartment, I dropped my handbag and my car keys on my coffee table and plopped down on the sofa in my living room. I kicked my shoes off my feet and snuggled up against the end pillow near the armrest. I lied there in silence while I thought back on the events from last night.

I saw my hit man as clear as day as he moved undetected into William's house from the side door. The hair on my skin stood up while the hit man and I made eye contact. The menacing look on his face was the look of death. There was no doubt in my mind that William's life wasn't about to end. The thought of his lifeless body leaving his residence in a body bag gave me a quick high until I got a call telling me otherwise. Something's got to happen to him and it needs to happen A.S.A.P.

Playing Dirty

The images of William's lifeless body faded to the detectives that were investigating his attack. The mere thought of them side eyeing me while they were questioning Tammy gave me chills. They made me think that they could see through me and that wasn't a good feeling. Thankfully I played it cool. I couldn't let them see me sweat. They'd harass me for sure then.

I hadn't realized that I had fallen asleep until my cell phone rang five hours later. I opened my eyes and was immediately blinded by the sunrays peering through the shutters covering my living room windows. I squinted my eyes and grabbed my phone from my handbag. When I looked at the caller ID I noticed the call was coming from Mrs. Elaine. My heart rate picked up speed. There was no doubt in my mind that she was calling to tell me that William had passed. This news was going to be music to my ears. "Hello," I finally said.

"Hi Kim, this is Mrs. Elaine. Did I catch you at a bad time?"

"No, ma'am." I replied as I sat straight up on the sofa.

"I'm gonna have the girls here at my house with me for the next few days while Tammy is at the hospital with William."

"That's good Mrs. Elaine. I'm sure they're happy with this arrangement." I told her.

"Well darling, I'm calling you because I have a doctor's appointment tomorrow and I would greatly appreciate it if you could come by and watch the girls while go out and make that appointment."

"Sure I can do that." I agreed.

"Okay great! Then I'll see you tomorrow around noon."

"Any word on William's condition?" I blurted out. I wasn't going to let Mrs. Elaine hang up her phone without giving me an update.

She let out a long sigh. "Nothing has change. His condition is still the same." She said.

"How is Tammy holding up?" I asked, even though I could care less. I figured I could never be too careful on these phones. With technology these days, anyone could be listening.

"She's a basket case so she could use all the prayers she can get."

"I see. So, how are you?"

"I'm living."

"And the girls?"

"They're good right now. God forbid if they lose their father. Losing two parents in a matter of weeks apart will devastate them. They may even go into deep depression."

"Well, let's pray for the best. Everything is going to work out fine." I tried assuring her.

Mrs. Elaine and I spoke for a few more minutes and then we both ended the call. After I hung up with her I hopped in the shower and then I got out and threw on a pair of sweat pants and a dark colored T-shirt. Immediately after I slipped on a pair of sneakers I grabbed my handbag, car keys and headed out to my car.

To get my mind off the botched job my hit man did on William, I went out to put eyes on the next bitch on my list. India Bates was the hoe's name. She was pretty little Asian and black chick with long, straight, black hair. She was also very petite. She had the frame of Jada Pinkett Smith. After she left my ex-husband's nightclub she got a gig at a high-end escort service agency. This chick was definitely about her paper. She went from fucking my husband to fucking a slew of rich motherfuckers for boatloads of cash. I found out her escort name was Pretty Patty. I couldn't tell you who came up with that lame ass name but according to my sources, she was a hot commodity amongst the company's white clients. She was making a good living for herself. She lived in an expensive high-rise apartment building and drove a late model 2-door Maserati. Sorry to say that life, as she knew it will all vanish before her eyes.

I knew she left her building everyday at 4:30 pm for work so I parked outside her apartment building thirty minutes before she made her departure. I sat in my car directly across the street and watched all the traffic coming and going from her building.

Like clockwork she exited the garage at approximately 4:30 and headed east on Shore Drive. I followed her for at least ten miles until she made her way onto the Oceanfront property of Atlantic Avenue. Most of the Atlantic Avenue area of Virginia Beach was home to wealthy, hedge fund investors and well sort after corporate and criminal attorneys. So when India pulled up to the valet area of the Sky Bar, I knew she was meeting a very wealthy client.

The Sky Bar was an elite, members only club for the high rollers in the Tidewater area so there was no way that I'd be able to spy on her from the inside. Instead of waiting around for her to leave the place I decided to get me a bite to eat from a nearby restaurant Catch 31.

Inside the restaurant, I took a seat at the bar, ordered a few cocktails and fried Calamari as an appetizer. While I basked in the ambiance of the restaurant, out of the blue comes this gentleman. "May I join you?" he asked.

When I looked up and saw how handsome this guy was, I smiled. "Sure," I replied.

He smiled back as he took a seat on the bar stool next to me. Then he extended his hand for a handshake. "I'm Julian." He introduced himself.

I shook his hand back and introduced myself as well. "So, what are you doing here by yourself?" he asked me.

"How do you know that I'm here alone?" I threw the question back at him.

"Because I've been watching you since you walked in here."

"So, you're a stalker?" I chuckled.

"Of course not. But look at how beautiful you are! It's impossible not to look at you." He explained. "So, are you married?" he continued.

"No. I'm divorced. And you?"

"Single. And I've never been married." He answered proudly. He was definitely a handsome guy. Kind of reminded me of the NBA player Kobe Bryant, but with far less height.

"So what do you do?" I wanted to know.

"I'm a bails bondsman."

"Really?! How long?"

"Eleven years give or take."

"How's it working out for you?"

"It pays the bills." He said, acting somewhat modest. "But enough about me, let's talk about you." He continued.

"What do you wanna know?"

"I wanna know what you do for a living?"

"Right now, nothing."

"So, how do you pay the bills?"

"My ex-husband takes care of my living expenses."

"Lucky you!"

"Trust me, it's not what you think."

"Do you have any kids?"

"Nope. I dodged that bullet. You?"

"No. So I guess I dodged that bullet too."

"Well that's one thing we have in common." I mentioned while I smiled.

This guy was somewhat intriguing. But like all the other guys in this town, I knew he had another side that would eventually rear it's ugly head after I let down my guard and give them some pussy.

"If I give you my number will you call me?" he asked me.

I hesitated for a moment and then I said, "Yeah, I guess."

He pulled his wallet from the inside of his jacket pocket and grabbed his business card from it. I looked at it after he handed it to me. "Oh, so you own your bail bondsman business?"

He cracked a half smile. "You can say that."

I stuck his business card in the side pocket of my handbag. "Do you come here a lot?"

"Once a week, maybe. What about you?"

"This is like my second time here."

"Hopefully, it won't be your last."

My smile widened. "It won't." I assured him.

"So, do you think I'd be able to see you again?" he asked me.

"That all depends," I said.

"On what?"

"Am I going to enjoy your company?"

"Of course. I won't have it any other way."

"Well then, there you have it." I said and then I took another sip of my drink. Before I sat my glass back down on the bar one of the waitresses approached Julian and I. "Excuse me, the gentleman sitting at the table by the door wanted me to give you this note." She said as she handed me a drink napkin with a few words scribbled on it. Julian and I looked in the direction were she was pointing but the table was empty. "Wait a minute, where did he go?" she asked aloud.

Julian and I hunched our shoulders. We had no fucking clue who the hell she was talking about. "It's okay, ma'am. Whoever it was is gone now." Julian spoke up while I looked down at the napkin to see what it said.

You aren't supposed to be here, the note read. Instantly, anxiety filled my entire body. After reading this note I knew the hit man was the one who had the waitress deliver it to me. And just like that, he vanished into thin air.

"Sorry about that," she apologized and walked away.

Julian turned his attention towards me while I balled the napkin up in my hand and shoved it down into my handbag. "So what did it say?" he asked me.

"Nothing important." I lied.

"It must've been a secret admirer." Julian joked.

"More like a stalker!" I commented and then I stood up from the barstool.

"You're leaving me already?" Julian sounded disappointed.

"I've got places to go and people to see." I lied to him once again. Whether he knew it or not, it was time for me to get out of here. My hit man had spoken. And when he speaks, I listen.

Julian walked me out to my car and before we said our goodbyes, he made me swear that I'd call him within the next 24-hours. So, I did and then we parted ways.

Time To Re-group

I was spooked the entire drive back to my apartment. The fact that the hit man was able to sneak up on me in that restaurant, didn't sit well with me. How the fuck did he get that close to me without me seeing him? I swear I was slipping hard. I was usually good about staying on point with my surroundings. But today of all days, I fucked up.

Aside from that, I knew what the note meant. The hit man wanted me out of the area because he was gearing up to rid me of India. I just hoped that he doesn't fumble the ball like he did with William. I can't let another mistake like that happen again. I paid good money for these hits, so the hit man better get his shit together or I'm going to get someone to finish him off.

Instead of going home, I decided to stop by my ex-husband's nightclub to see how everything was going. He and I weren't on the best terms but at least we were speaking. When I pulled up in the parking lot I saw his Aston Martin parked in his designated parking space. One part of me wanted to key his fucking car up while the other part of me didn't want me to waist my time.

He was a miserable, cheating ass bastard with no heart or respect for anyone. So, in due time he'd get what's coming for him.

It was 7:00 in the evening so the club had little to no patrons inside. My ex-husband was nowhere insight, but that didn't shock me. I figured he'd be in his office getting his dick sucked by one of his waitresses. Getting his dicked sucked at work was his favorite pastime.

"Where is Drake?" I asked the pretty, young chick standing behind the bar. She looked too young to be a bartender but when I thought about all the other girls Drake hired in the past, they looked younger than this one. He was a fucking sucker for young hoes. They seemed to always tickle his fucking fancy.

This Aaliyah look-alike smiled and said, "It think he's back in his office. Would you like for me to go and get him?"

"Oh no baby, you tend to your customer. I'm his ex-wife. I know where his office is." I told her and started walking in the direction of his office.

Halfway to Drake office, he mysteriously appeared in the hallway right outside his office door. I could see the smile on his face just as clear as day. "Whatcha' so happy for?" I asked him as I continued to walk towards him.

He started walking towards me as well. "I'm happy about life." He replied as his smile widened.

"Cut out the bullshit!" I said nonchalantly as I folded my arms across my chest.

"What bullshit Kim?" He asked as he tried to extend his arms to give me a hug.

I took a step backwards. "Don't touch me with those hands. Only God knows whose pussy you've been digging in with those things." I commented sarcastically.

"Come on now, stop busting my balls and tell me what brought you by my fine establishment." He got straight to the point.

"I was just in the neighborhood and decided to drop by." I explained.

Before he could utter another word his office door opened and out came a cute, young girl who looked to be in her early 20's. He and I both looked in her direction. "Something's never change with you." I commented while I looked the young lady from head to toe.

"Sorry, did I interrupt something?" she asked.

"Oh no honey, I'm just the ex-wife. You're fine." I announced. I wanted the bitch to know that I wasn't some side hoe, but that I used to be the HBIC once upon of time.

"What do you need Casey?" Drake asked her.

"I was just going to the bar to get a drink." She told him as she made her way towards us. She was beautiful. Her brown skin was flawless. Her was short with huge locks of curls. Her body was shaped like an hourglass. She definitely had it going on. For a minute there I felt somewhat jealous. I mean, how is it that this bastard is able to move on and bring women in his life that was younger and more attractive than me? What kind of bullshit is that? I swear I should've cut his dick off the first time I caught him cheating on me. Maybe then I wouldn't be having these freaking feelings for him. Life wasn't fair to me at all.

"What is she like 18-years-old?" I asked sarcastically. I wanted to embarrass him and fuck with her at the same time. And guess what? It worked. The dumb bitch took the bait.

"No, I'm 25. But you definitely look like you're pushing 40." She interjected sarcastically as she slid by Drake and I and headed into the direction of the bar.

"And you look like you've sucked over 40 dicks." I barked. How dare that bitch come for me like that? Did she know who the fuck I was? I knew one thing, she'd better keep her fucking mouth close or she's going to end up like all those other bitches that fucked Drake. Fucking hoe!

"Really, Kim?! Was that even necessary?" Drake spat. He was not pleased with how I came down on his new girlfriend. But I could care less about how pleased he was. I was a woman scorned so he had no other choice but to deal with my actions.

"What did I say wrong? She did look like she was about 17 or 18 years old." I challenged him in a cynical way.

"You know it's against the law to have anyone in the club under 21. So, why even take me there?"

"Look, I'm not trying to take you anywhere. I told you I was in the neighborhood and decided to drop by to see you."

"Are you here for money?"

"Of course not! I'm good."

"Well then if you're good then let me walk you to your car." He offered and then he began escorting me towards the front entrance of the nightclub.

The moment we stepped outside into the parking lot he wanted to know the details surrounding my best friend's ex-husband's shooting incident. "You didn't see it on the news?" I asked him.

"Yeah, sort of. But I'm sure you know what really happened?"

"According to Mariah's mother, somebody entered into his home while he was in his home office and shot him. The paramedics rushed him to the hospital where he's in ICU in a medically induced coma."

"Oh damn! I didn't know that he was in a coma."

"Yeah, he is. And from the looks of it, he may not come out of it."

"I know his new wife is about to lose her mind."

"Yeah, she is. But what wife wouldn't?"

"So how are you holding up since Mariah passed away?"

"I'm taking things one day at a time."

"I still can't believe that's she's gone."

"Neither can I," I agreed and then pulled my car keys from my handbag. "Let me get out of here."

"You sure you're alright?" he asked me once again.

"Yes, I'm good." I smiled. "Take care of yourself. And don't let those young girls take all of your money and run your old ass crazy!"

"Don't worry about me. I've got everything under control." He smiled back.

Instead of replying, I shook my head with disgust. Drake used to be the love of my life until he betrayed me. Before seeing him today, I thought I had gotten over him. But after seeing that bitch come out of his office, my old wounds opened. All the hurt and pain that plagued me once before had resurfaced. So, the question is, will I ever get over that cheating asshole? Whatever my answer was, I knew I wouldn't be able to say it now, especially while my mind was so clouded with everything else I had going on. In a perfect world,

I'd just snap my fingers and rid myself with any feelings I had left in my heart concerning him.

To get away from his bullshit, I got into my car and headed home. This was the only place I could go to and get some sanity. I had a lot of things I needed to think about before I made my next move.

Home Sweet Home

I knew I had to get up in the morning and head over to Mrs. Elaine's house to watch the girls, so I took a quick shower, threw on a tank top, a pair of black, box-boxer shorts and then I hopped in the bed. For some reason, my bed felt good as hell tonight. It was so plush and comfy. The only thing I was missing was a man. The man I had in mind was my new friend Julian. Our introduction was the best so when I decide to call him, I truly hope that I am not wasting my time.

Before I drifted off to sleep, my mind quickly reminded me about the note the hit man addressed to me at the restaurant earlier. I also wondered if he had really told me to leave that place because he was about to handle his business with India. Whatever his note meant, it started bothering me to no end. Normally I'd turn on the TV to see if there was a special news bulletin about a murder but I decided against it this time. I noticed how I torture myself when I'm trying to find out if my hits have been carried out. Some may call it micromanaging while others called it being controlling. Whichever hat I wore, it didn't give me the peace I needed to carry me from day to day. I finally found out what I'd been missing, after I had a drink with that guy from earlier. He was a sweetheart. And maybe he could be the one that could teach me how to love again. I guess time would tell.

The following morning I got up, showered, got dressed and headed over to Mrs. Elaine's house. She met me at the front door after I called her and told her that I was outside. She gave me a warm smile and a gigantic hug after she let me into the house. "Thank you so much for coming over at such short notice."

"Don't mention it. You know I'm always here for you." I told her.

"The girls are in the kitchen eating breakfast." She mentioned after she closed the front door.

I walked down the hallway that led to the kitchen. Mrs. Elaine followed in my footsteps. "Good morning young ladies," I greeted them.

"Good morning to you too." They both replied in unison.

I sat in a chair across from them while Mrs. Elaine grabbed her keys and handbag from the nearby kitchen counter. "You girls better behave while Ms. Kim is looking after you." Mrs. Elaine warned them.

"Don't worry Mrs. Elaine, they'll be good. Right girls?" I chimed in.

The girls agreed so Mrs. Elaine kissed them both and headed to her doctor's appointment. Immediately after she left, I sat at the table and made small talk with the girls. I wanted to know how they were feeling especially after losing their mother to suicide while their father is lying in an Intensive Care Unit fighting for his life. "So, how are you girls feeling?" I asked in a cheerful kind of way.

"I'm okay." Tasha said.

"What about you Tisha?" I questioned her.

"I guess I'm okay." She replied nonchalantly.

"Do you girls miss your mother?" I continued to question them.

"Yeah. We miss her a lot." Tasha spoke up.

Tisha agreed by nodding her head.

"What do you girls miss most about your mother?"

"I miss when she used to take us to get gelato." Tisha said.

"Yeah, me too. That was one of our favorite places." Tasha agreed.

"What else?" I continued to probe them. It felt good to hear them express their feelings about their mother.

"Well, I like when she used to take us to get our nails done." Tasha answered.

"Yeah, I did too because she would let us get any design we wanted." Tisha chimed in.

"Anything else?"

"I know I'm gonna miss when she used to let us help her bake our birthday cakes." Tasha mentioned.

"Yeah, I'm gonna miss that too." Tasha agreed.

"How do you two feel about your father being in the hospital? Does it make you sad?" I wanted to know.

"Yeah, it makes me sad." Tisha answered first.

"Why?" I probed more.

"Because I think he's gonna die like our mom did." Tisha continued.

"Do you know how to pray?" I asked them both.

"Yeah," Tisha said, while Tasha nodded her head.

"Well, before you go to bed at night get on your knees and pray and ask God to make him better. God listens to little girls like you two." I told them.

"Think it'll work?"

"Nothing beats a failure but a try." I replied. But deep in my heart I wanted the exact opposite. I wanted that bastard to die. He didn't deserve to take another breath especially after the way he treated my best friend. So, if I had my way, I'd pull the plug on his ass faster than his new wife could blink her eyes.

The twins and I headed into the family room to watch a few TV shows but in between commercials I had more questions for them to answer. "How do you girls like your dad's new wife? Is she nice to you?" I asked them.

"Sometimes." Tasha replied first.

"What about you Tisha? Is she nice to you?"

"She's okay, I guess. Sometimes she gets on my nerves though." Tisha said.

"How does she get on your nerves?"

"Lately she's been trying to act like she's our mother but I don't pay her any attention. Because she'll never be like our mom." Tisha continued.

"Your mother would smile right now if she heard you say that. Remember no one will ever take the place of your mother. She was a very special lady. And she loved you girls so much. So, always keep a special place in your heart for her."

"We do." Tisha assured me, while Tasha nodded.

The girls and I talked a little more until their favorite show "2 Broke Girls" came on. Every one of us went mum from the time the show started until it finished. I looked at them several times and wondered how they really felt about their mother's death. Not too mention, that their father was on his way out too. I swear my heart went out to these two beautiful little girls. They needed their mother, not their heartless ass father. I just wished he'd do all of us a favor and die already. His services are no longer needed here on earth. UGH!

Too Close For Comfort

Mrs. Elaine came back to the house about an hour and a half later and invited me on her newly built patio in the back of her house. We talked briefly about her plans for the girls and their father's condition. For the life of me, I couldn't figure out why she wanted William to live so badly. He was the fucking reason why her daughter committed suicide. He was also the reason why she couldn't spend time with her grandkids. So, where was all of this pity coming from? "I prayed all night long that God would reverse William's condition. Those girls need at least one of their parents here on this earth." She expressed.

"Don't you blame him for Mariah's suicide? And let's not forget how he tried to keep you from spending time with your daughter's kids." I reminded her.

"If God forgives me, then I must forgive him." She replied.

"Yeah, and God also said don't be fooled too." I responded sarcastically.

"Kim, you just gotta look at life a little differently. You can't be mad at someone when they do you wrong. Forgive them and move on. Because if you don't, then they have the power."

"Well, I guess they're gonna have the power because I wouldn't be able to forgive someone right after they stabbed me in my back. Now way." I told her.

After I expressed my grievances about William and how I believed that if he hadn't treated Mariah the way he did, then she'd still be here. Mrs. Elaine on the other hand, gave me some off the wall explanation about how it was God's will for things to happen the way that they did. But I wasn't trying to hear that bullshit that lady was talking about. God doesn't want people walking around here committing suicide. It was apparent that she was smoking something because only someone high would say something as dumb as that.

I swear I had had enough of Mrs. Elaine lip services and decided that it was time that I leave. "I'll call you later to check on you." I assured her.

She gave me a kiss on the cheek and told me that she'd be waiting on my call. She also promised to call me if William's condition changed for the worst. Now that was a phone call I wanted to wait around for. William's ass needed to go.

On my way back to my house I picked up my cell phone and called Julian. Shockingly, he answered on the fifth ring. "Hello," he said.

"I'm surprised you answered. I was about to hang up." I told her.

"Well, I'm glad you didn't." I replied.

"Did I catch you at a bad time?" I wanted to know.

"I was on the other end talking to the wife of a new client I'm about to go and bail out."

"Oh I'm sorry, take care of your business and call me back."

"No, she's gone. I can talk." He assured me.

"Are you sure?" I asked him. I had to put on the act like I wasn't anxious to talk to him.

"I told you I'm good. So, stop trying to get me off the phone."

"I'm not trying to get you off the phone."

"Good. So, tell me how your day went?"

"Well, I had to run a couple of errands and then I babysat my best friend's little girls for a few hours. Other than that, it was pretty simple."

"So, you like kids?"

"Of course, I love kids."

"Do you plan to have some one day?"

"I don't think having kids is in the cards for me."

"You never know." He commented.

"I won't hold my breath."

"Well, can you tell me when I'd be able to see you again?" He got straight to the point.

"I don't know. I mean, it depends on what you have in mind." I flirted with the idea.

"What about dinner?"

"When?"

"Tomorrow night."

"Where?"

"What about the Italian restaurant Bravo's in Town Center?"

"Bravo's, huh?"

"Yeah. Have you been there?"

"A couple times."

"So that means you like it?"

"Yeah, I like their food."

"So, you're saying, yes?"

I hesitated for a moment and then I said, "Yes."

He was very happy that I had given him the green light. The only reason I accepted his invitation for dinner was because I needed a little distraction from everything that was going on around me. I knew I would eventually lose my damn mind trying to keep tabs on all the hits I put out. My micro-managing behavior was getting a little out of control so having a new man around could definitely take my mind off a lot of things.

"So what time is our dinner date?" I asked him.

"How does 7:00 p.m. sound?"

"That's great time. So, I guess I'll see you there," I said.

"I guess you will." He added.

We talked for a few more minutes until he got another call for his bail services. I insisted that he handle his business and give me a call the next day. After he assured me that he would we said our goodbyes.

Immediately after I hung up with him, I couldn't help but think about how handsome and manly he was. I got chills just thinking about him holding me in those big arms he had. Having someone new to talk to seemingly gave me a burst of energy. It was the energy I needed to live another day.

Checking On My Investment

I got up the next morning earlier than usual. For some reason I couldn't shake the fact that I hadn't heard anything about any new murders and this had me concerned. I rolled over towards the lampstand next to my bed and grabbed my cell phone from it. I pressed speed dial to get my hit man on the phone but he didn't answer. I was shocked because he always answered my calls. I figured something must've been wrong, so I called him again. To no avail, he didn't answer his phone the second time. Panic instantly shot through my entire body. My mind started racing and my palms started sweating. I couldn't wrap my mind around why wasn't this fucking guy answering my calls. I mean, had he been arrested? Or had he just not handled my business and fucked up another hit? I knew one thing, if the latter was true, then I was going to have to take matters into my own hands.

Several hours passed and I called the hit man again but I still got no answer. Before putting my cell phone down I called Mrs. Elaine to check up on William's condition. One of the twins answered her cell phone. "Hello," the little girl said.

"Hi sweetheart, this is Auntie Kim. Where is your grandmother?" I replied.

"She's in her room. Hold on a minute and I'll get her." She told me.

I heard her little feet running at a pretty fast pace and then I heard her cute little voice announce to her grandmother that I was on the phone. A couple of seconds later Mrs. Elaine spoke into the phone. "Hi there," she said.

"How are you Mrs. Elaine?"

"If my arthritis wasn't bugging me, I'll be in good shape. But never mind about me, how are you doing this morning?"

"I guess I'm okay. But there's not a day that goes by and I don't think about Mariah."

"I think about her everyday too. It gets so bad that I have to pray and ask God to comfort me when I start to get depressed."

"Don't worry. It'll get better." I told her and then I changed the subject. "So, have you heard anything else about William's condition?"

"No. I spoke with Tammy this morning and she said that his condition is the same."

"I know she's going through it."

"I'm sure she is." Mrs. Elaine agreed.

"Are you taking the girls up there to see him today?"

"Yes, I'm going to drive them up there around noon."

"Well, give Tammy my best."

"I sure real." Mrs. Elaine assured me.

After I said a few more words to her, I ended the call. I wasn't too pleased to hear that William's condition hadn't changed. I wished he'd die already. I can't let him come back and live a normal fucking life. Mariah was dead. So that meant, he deserved the same fate.

←—————————————————————→

I grabbed my keys and left my apartment. I couldn't figure why I hadn't been able to get my hit man on the phone. This shit was starting to fuck with my head. The fact that I hadn't heard or seen anything on TV about that last chick I followed to the Sky Bar didn't bode over well with me either. I had to find out what was going on. And being in the house wasn't cutting it for me.

I drove back to the expensive ass high-rise building Ms. India Bates lived in thirty minutes before she normally departed to head to work. I parked my car across the street and watched all the traffic that came and went. I listened to my favorite R&B CD while I monitored everything moving. While I surveyed the front entrance of the building and the exit way of the garage, I saw some very rich, but interesting characters.

The first person I laid eyes on was this older looking white bitch. She stood outside while the valet driver fetched her car. She held her poodle in one arm while a red leather Hermes' Birkin draped over her other arm. She looked like money. She even looked like she hadn't worked a day in her life. There was no doubt in my mind that she was a kept woman. I surely remembered those days. Drake took care of me. But once those sideline bitches came lurking, his priorities changed. I swear I wished I was a little wiser when I was married to him. I sure would've walked away with a lot more money than I got.

The next person I laid my eyes on was an older gentleman. He looked like he could be an attorney. He was a well-groomed white guy dressed in a tailor made suit. I could see his $1,000 red bottom dress shoes from 500 feet away. Immediately after the valet driver handed the gentleman the keys to his late model Porsche Carrera, he got into his car and sped off into the sunset. It was like something you'd see in a movie about a bank robbery and their getaway driver.

Not too long after the white guy drove away, a young woman that looked around the same age India walked out of the main entrance of the apartment building and stood alongside the curb. She wasn't as pretty as India, but she looked like new money as she sported her Chanel boy bag, cushion cut diamond earrings and the matching cushion cut diamond ring on her finger. And when her significant other walked out of the building and accompanied her at the curb, I instantly knew that he was the one that gave her those lavish gifts. Several minutes later, their black, G-Class, Mercedes SVU was chauffeured to the front of the building by one of the valet drivers. The guy handed the valet driver some cash and then the couple climbed inside their vehicle and sped off.

I think I watched at least twenty or more people get in and out of their cars while I waited for Ms. India to show her face. And before I knew it, and hour passed and I saw no sign of India. So where was she? Was she in fact dead?

I sat there in my car, scratching my head, trying to figure out what the hell was going on. I pulled my cell phone out and dialed my hit man's number once again. But I still got no answer. "What the fuck you doing dude?!" I spat. The fact that this guy wasn't answering my calls was getting underneath my fucking skin. Why the fuck am I not able to get in contact with this guy? Was he trying to avoid me or something? Had he taken my money and left town without taking care of my business? Shit! I needed some answers. And I needed them now.

Being as though I couldn't handle not knowing what was going on, I made a hasty decision by making a trip inside of India's apartment building. I decided that I was going to get some answers with or without the hit man.

I hopped out of my car and dashed across the street towards the building. There were three valet drivers outside helping the residents of the building so I just slipped by them and opened the glass door. A doorman greeted me. He was a huge black man that reminded me of the deceased actor Duncan Clarke from the Green Mile. "Good afternoon!" he said.

I smiled. "Good afternoon!" I replied while I tried to skirt by him.

"Visiting someone?" he wanted to know.

"Ummm, yeah," I said clearing my throat, "I'm here to see my friend." I continued, hoping and praying he wouldn't ask me for a name.

"And who might that be?" He pressed the issue.

"India," I said, without even realizing I uttered her name.

"I haven't seen her today." The doorman said.

My heart sunk into the pit of my stomach. From that point, something on the inside of me confirmed the answer I was looking for, but then my mind kicked in overdrive and forced me to press the doorman for information. "I'm here to pick her up, so could you call up to her place and let her know I'm here?" I said, hoping he'd take the bait.

"I don't think she's in her apartment. But let me check." He continued and then he escorted me to the front desk, which was located a few feet away from the glass front doors. There was a white woman standing behind the desk dressed in business attire. "Hi Jake, how can I help you?" she smiled and asked.

"Has Ms. Bates valeted her car today?" he asked her.

"Hold on and let me check." She replied.

She hit a couple of keys on her keypad and then she searched the computer monitor. My heart raced at a speed that felt like it was about to burst through my chest cavity. Sweat started seeping through my pores and the palms of my hands started itching like crazy. I swear, it felt like I was about to have a fucking nervous breakdown.

"The last time she valeted her car was yesterday evening. And I don't see when she returned with it. But that doesn't mean that she didn't come home." the woman explained.

"Could you ring her apartment to see if she's there?" I asked her, even though I really didn't want her to do it. The fear of India answering the phone to here apartment and asking the desk clerk for my name started weighing heavily on me. But I couldn't turn back now. I knew I'd look very suspicious if I did it, so I stood there calmly and waited for the woman to make the call. While we waited, the doorman insisted that I was in good hands with the clerk and then he stepped off and walked back towards the front entrance.

The woman held the phone up to her left ear for a few seconds and then her facial expression changed. "Hello Ms. Bates," she started off and then she fell silent. Instantly, I became sick. The fact that India answered the phone took me on a world wind of emotions. I wanted to run away. But then I decided against it. I knew I had to play it cool before I blew my cover.

The clerk looked at me and said, "I thought I was talking her but I actually got her voicemail," she whispered as she covered the receiver with the palm of her hand.

"You can hang up. I don't need you to leave a message." I insisted.

"Are you sure?" she whispered once again.

"Yes, I'm sure," I assured her.

Thankfully, she took my word for it and ended the call.

"I think I know where she's at." I lied and started walking backwards. I knew it was time for me to get my ass from out of here.

"Wanna leave your name and a number? I'll definitely make sure she gets it." She asked me.

"No, I'm good." I said and then I turned around and left the building.

As soon as I walked outside, I dashed towards my car. I couldn't get out of there quick enough. I knew without a doubt now that India was dead. But where was she and why hadn't I been able to get in touch with the hit man? What was really going on with him?

I Need Some Fucking Answers

Instead of going home, I made a detour and headed to the hospital to see William. For the life of me I wanted that motherfucker dead, if he wasn't already. I figured that I might have to take matters into my own hand.

Immediately after I parked my car in the hospital's parking garage I made my way inside the hospital. The trip to ICU was fairly quick. I was there in a matter of three minutes. To my surprise Tammy wasn't in the room when I walked in. There was a nurse accompanying William. She was monitoring the ventilating machine. I spoke to her while I closed the door behind me. She looked up at me, spoke back and then she carried on with what she was doing.

"How is he doing?" I inquired.

"Are you a relative?" she answered without looking back.

"His deceased ex-wife was my best friend, so I'm considered family." I told her.

"Well, his wife spoke to the doctor not too long ago. And she just stepped out for a moment to get something to eat from the cafeteria. So she should be back at any minute," she told me. In other words, she wasn't trying to tell me a damn thing. She wanted me to wait to get any information I needed from Tammy. End of story.

"Oh okay, thank you." I said. When in reality, I wanted to tell her to stop being a bitch. In my mind, she could've told me what was going on with William's ass. I mean, it isn't a secret that he's in a fucking coma and the only thing that's keeping him alive is that fucking ventilator.

I took a seat in a chair next to William's bed. I looked at him from head to toe. He looked sound to sleep with all the needles and tubes attached to him. I swear, I wanted to snuff him out with his bed pillow. The fact that the doctors and nurses were doing everything in their power to keep this man alive made me sick to my stomach. Hate instantly engulfed me while I gave him a hard stare. My blood started boiling inside my veins too. I had no desire whatsoever to see this bastard come out of this alive. He needed to suffer the same fate as my best friend Mariah. I figured maybe I'd stick around for a while and pray for his demise, it'll happen.

After the nurse logged some data onto William's chart, she took the medical file with her and exited the room. I sat there alone with William and it immediately felt like the room was closing in around me. The energy became thick. It felt like a dark cloud was looming over my head. I looked at him with the most disgusted expression I could muster up. "I just wish you would fucking die!" I said, gritting my teeth.

"You don't deserve to be alive. You're a mean as hell and you're a fucking piece of shit!" I continued, cringing at the sight of this maggot. I stood up on my feet and leaned forward to get in his face. "I fucking hate you! So die why don't you!" I uttered, while grinding my teeth.

"What did you just say?" said a voice a few feet away.

Shocked by an unexpected presence, I looked up from William and saw that the same nurse had reentered the room. A feeling of warmness overpowered my body. It felt like I had a hot flash. My mind started scrambling and nothing made sense to me until she spoke once again. "Are you going to tell me what you just said to that patient? she pressed the issue.

"What did it sounded like I said?" I threw the question back at her. I knew I sounded a bit defensive, but I needed to know what she thought she heard me say.

"It sounded like you asked him why don't he die!" she came back at me.

"Well, you're wrong. I told him that he needed to come alive." I lied. I gave the nurse a sincere expression while I lied to her.

She hesitated for a moment while she gathered her thoughts. And because of this, I knew that her mind could go either way, which was why I figured I might need to be a little more convincing. With William's coma incident still under investigation, I couldn't afford for the nurse to blow my cover to the cops so I went into overdrive. "Listen nurse, I know that you don't know me or anything about my relationship with this man right here," I began to explain while I pointed at William, "but I can assure you that everyone who does know he and I, know that I have nothing but love for him. He's the father of my deceased best friend's little girls. I've been in this man's life for at least fifteen years so trust me; you don't have to second-guess anything that I said. It's all love between he and I. And that's my word." I said, concluding my explanation.

Before the nurse could respond, Tammy walked back into the room. Anxiety immediately took over my body once again. I didn't know whether to run out of there or stay and plead my case. "What's going on?" Tammy asked, as she tried to close the room door behind herself.

"Oh nothing," I interjected, "she walked in the room while I was talking to William and she thought I said something so I cleared it up."

"What did you say?" Tammy wanted to know.

"I was just telling him to come live because the girls need him." I lied once again. The whole scene felt like I was in court and on trial for my life.

"Oh, okay." Tammy replied and sat the bag of food she was carrying down on tray table next to William's bed.

The nurse gave me the side eye look like she still had doubts about what I said. And instead of voicing it, she shrugged it off her shoulders and walked back over to the ventilator and started monitoring the machine again. Seeing this took a load off my shoulders. I just pray that she doesn't bring this incident back up and especially to the cops.

Tammy made a few inquires to the nurse about William's condition. After she told Tammy that his condition was the same and nothing changed, I could see the pain Tammy was dealing with all over her face. She couldn't mask it if she tried. I walked over to her and gave her a hug. I wanted to show some compassion just in case the nurse was watching me. This whole act of mine was critical and it had to go off without a hitch.

"Don't worry about what you see. God can change this thing around for William quicker than we can blink our eyes." I encouraged her while I embraced her.

She hugged me back and thanked me for comforting her. "Don't me, thank God. He's the one that's gonna make William wake up out of that coma and get out of that bed." I continued with a few more words of encouragement.

"Thank you so so much!" Tammy said once more.

"So, have you spoken with the detectives anymore?" I changed the subject as soon as the nurse left the room.

"Yes, they came by earlier today."

"So, what are they saying?"

"They really weren't saying much. But they had a lot more questions they wanted to ask me."

"Do they even have a suspect?" I inquired. I wanted to know. I figured if they did, then that was probably why I hadn't heard from my hit man.

"If they do they didn't share that information with me."

"So, what kind of questions did they ask you?" I pressed her.

"They basically wanted me to go over the events that took place after I heard William struggling with the intruder down in his office."

"That's it?"

"Yep," she replied and then she turned her attention back towards William.

"Don't worry about it. Who's ever responsible for this will pay for it. You just watch." I assured her.

I sat there with Tammy until the shift changed and believe me it was torture watching that nigga lying there like he was asleep. But what really aggravated me was how Tammy was hovering over him like he was a prize possession and talked about how good of a person he was. He was an arrogant bastard in my eyes. And I can honestly say that he got what he deserved.

On my way out of the room, I wished Tammy the best and told her I'd be praying for William's full recovery, a lie I made of course. She thanked me once again and then we parted ways.

It seemed like the moment I stepped out of that hospital room, the dark cloud that loomed over me had disappeared. The disgusting feeling of watching William lying in his bed like he was asleep drove me fucking crazy. I knew one thing; I vowed that if he hadn't died before the week was over, I was going to pull the fucking plug myself.

The agony I felt because of the botched job my hit man did triggered me to pull out my cell phone and dial his number again. I really needed to get some shit off my chest concerning the fucked up job he did. Not only that, the fact that I hadn't been able to contact needed to be addressed as well. And even though I had all of this shit built up inside of me, I knew there was a fat chance that he'd answer my call.

I put the phone up to my ear after I dialed his number. I sat there in my car, waiting for the voicemail to pick up because I knew he wasn't going to answer. But guess what? I was wrong. Surprisingly, he answered this time. "Yes," he said.

"I need to talk to you now. Call me back on this line." I instructed him. Like clockwork the hit man call me right back. I answer the phone on the first ring. "Hello," I wasted no time to say.

"What can I do for you?"

"Where have you been? I've been trying to contact you."

"Where I've been shouldn't be of any importance to you."

"Well, can you tell me why the fuck William isn't dead?" I barked.

"Don't worry about that. I will take care of it."

"When?" I snapped.

"Very soon," he replied nonchalantly.

"Well it better be very soon, because he's in a coma and he can wake up at any given moment."

"I understand your concern." He continued in a nonchalant manner.

"Well you should because I paid you a lot of money

to get rid of him some time ago."

"Don't worry, I'm gonna handle it."

"What about India?"

"What about her?"

"Have you taken care of her?"

"She's a done deal."

"Well how come I hadn't seen anything about her on the news?"

"Because that's the way I wanted it." He replied. "And by the way, if you don't want to become a murder suspect, I'm advising you to stay clear of the rest of the women I have on my list."

"Point taken." I said.

"If that's it, then I must go." He said and without further notice he disconnected our call.

Can I Get a Rain Check?

Later that evening, I fell tired so lied down on the sofa to get a quick nap before it was time to get ready for my dinner date with Julian. Unfortunately, I couldn't close my eyes. After tossing and turning for the next fifteen minutes, I decided to call it quits. But then when I tried to stand up on my feet, I couldn't move my body off the sofa. I was literally burnt out. From that point, I knew going out to dinner wasn't going to be a good idea. So, I practiced one excuse after the other in my head until I felt like it was convincing enough to tell it to Julian. Once I had my lie down packed I reached over to the coffee table and grabbed ahold of my cell phone. I dialed his number and waited for him to pick it up.

"Hi, beautiful!" He said.

"Hi, Julian."

"Are you ready for our date tonight?"

"Well, that's what I was calling you about."

"Uhh oh, don't tell me you're calling to cancel on me."

"Julian, I am so tired right now. And if I go out with you tonight, I'm going to be the worst date ever."

"What's wrong? Did you have a rough day?"

"I did a lot of running around all day, so I'm sure you can imagine how bad my feet hurt right now."

"Well, I'll tell you what, if you let me come by your house I'll cook dinner for you."

I hesitated before I answered him. He noticed it to. "Come on now, I'm not gonna bite. And I'm a nice and respectful gentleman. I will not become a stalker or any of that craziness. You have my word." He continued.

"Okay, well I guess I can do it this once. But you better be on your best behavior."

"I promise, I will." He assured me. "So, what is your favorite food?"

"Anything that includes pasta."

"Well, I have the perfect dish for you."

"I will taste good."

"It will, don't you worry about that. So, text me your address and I'll see you later." He said.

Immediately after our call ended, I text him my home address. Once he confirmed that he had it, I placed my cell phone back on the coffee table and forced myself to get out and take a shower. I wasn't going to let Julian see me like this. Nor did I want him smell that outdoors smell all my clothes. I hadn't had a man over to my house for some time now. So I had to make this night special. I wanted to look special and smell special. And that's what I intended to do.

Julian showed up at my front door at 7 o'clock on the dot with food in tow. When I opened the door he gave me this huge smile. "Well, hello." He said.

I smile back. "And hello to you too." I said and then I stepped to the side so he could come into my home.

"You have a beautiful home." He complemented me.

"Thank you," I replied graciously while I took a long look at his backside. His shoulders were broad, his height is perfect and his butt was just the right size. But what really got my attention was that he smelled so good.

After I closed the door and locked it, I escorted him to the kitchen. I helped him place the bags onto the island. "I thought you were going to cook for me." I mentioned after I peeked inside the bags.

"Well, I kind of lied to you." He said with a naughty facial expression.

I folded my arms and waited for him to explain himself. "I'm waiting," I said, with a slight smirk.

"I really can't cook. But I figured if I had told you that, I would not have been able to see you tonight."

I playfully slapped him on his arm. He flinched a little bit. "You are something else Julian."

"Look at how beautiful you are. You can't blame me for wanting to see you." He reasoned.

I continued to smile, but more bashfully. "You better not lie to me again." I warned him playfully. "So, where did you go?" I questioned him.

"I went to an Italian spot right by my office. I heard their pasta was the best in town so I stopped by there to check them out." He answered.

"So, what did you get?" I wondered aloud.

Julian pulled the first container of food out of the bag and placed it on the kitchen island. "This is shrimp scampi." He told me. "And this is pasta pomodora with Italian sausage." He continued after he placed the second container next to the first one.

"Oh my God! They both smell so good."

"Well, I'll tell you what, I'll give you some portions of both so you can see which one you like better."

"Sounds like a plan to me." I commented while I rubbed the palm of my hands together.

I grabbed a couple of plates from dishwasher and two forks from the silverware drawer. Julian fixed our plates while I grabbed two champagne glasses from the kitchen cabinet. "So, we're drinking out of the champagne glasses, huh?" He smiled.

I smiled back at him. "This is a dinner date, right?" I questioned him.

"I was hoping it was," he commented.

"Well, there you go." I replied and then I grabbed a bottle of Veuve Clicquot from the refrigerator.

Julian and I took a seat across from each other at my dining room table. I lit the candles I had sat out before Julian arrived and from there the mood was set. I was surprised when Julian said a prayer before we ate. For some odd reason, this was very attractive to me.

While we ate, we talked about our likes and dislikes, where we've traveled and places we'd love to go. But when Julian wanted to know who initiated my divorce, I froze up. I didn't want to seem like a woman scorned. That type of behavior will scare men away. "I don't wanna waste your time with that nonsense. Let's talk about your last relationship." I threw the question back at him.

"What do you wanna know?"

I giggled. "You weren't supposed to say that."

Julian gave me a dumbfounded expression. "What else was I supposed to say?" he asked me.

"You were supposed to say that you didn't want to talk about anyone you've dealt with." I coached him.

"Listen, my life is pretty simple and it's like an open book. So, I have nothing to hide. And I don't have any regrets."

"Well, I have a ton of regrets and I'm sorry but I don't like talking about them." I told him in a nonchalant manner.

"Okay, I can respect that." He agreed and then he changed the subject. "So, are you enjoying your food?" he wanted to know.

"You see it's half gone don't you?" I chuckled, using my right hand to cover my mouth so he doesn't see the food in my mouth.

"Good. I'm glad."

After dinner Julian and I retired to the living room. It was my idea to sip a couple more glasses of Veuve Clicquot while we watched a movie on Netflix. Julian was happy about spending more time with me so it didn't matter to him if we'd sit at the kitchen table and watch each other for the rest of night. "Let's watch the new movie with Idris Elba in it." I suggested.

"Which movie is that?" He wondered aloud.

"It's called Beast of Nations and I hear it's good."

"Well, that's what we'll watch then." He agreed. So, I navigated through the search menu of the Netflix home screen and when I found Idris Elba's new movie I clicked on it and started the play button. I got a little closer to Julian while we watched the movie. The cologne he had on was intoxicating. That alone made him more desirable than ever.

Thirty minutes into the movie he put his arms around me so I snuggled up against him. I swear it felt really good to finally have a man hold me. The fact that he smelled good made it even easier to be next to him. Before I knew it, I had fallen asleep. He woke me up after the movie had gone off. His touch was so gentle. "Hey sweetheart, the movie just went off," he told me.

I readjusted my eyes to see him because my vision was blurry. I smiled immediately after I zoomed in on his handsome face. "I'm sorry for falling asleep on you." I apologized as I sat straight up on the sofa.

"Don't worry about me. I'm good. Just being able to spend some time with you is enough for me."

I smiled. "That's so sweet of you to say."

"Trust me, I mean it." He said and then gave me the most handsome expression he could muster up.

"You know your smile is infectious?" I commented.

"And so are you," he replied, giving me the stare of a lifetime. Even though it was dark in the room and the only light we had illuminated from the TV, I could still see how intoxicating his eyes were. It felt like he could see right through me. We had a connection and it was evident. I just wished that this moment could last forever.

I was so caught up in Julian's gaze that I didn't realize he had kissed me until our lips touched. I swear the kiss was magical. Sparks between us exploded like fireworks. So when he tried to pull away from me, as I grabbed him by his neck and pulled him back towards me. Once again our lips touched and all kinds of explosions went off. The way he took control of this moment was something I had not experienced before. And before I knew it, I allowed him to climb on top of me and do with me what he wanted. Together he and I were sprawled across my sofa, caressing, rubbing, kissing and feeling each other all over. "Mmmmm, I wanna feel you inside of me," I began to beg him between kisses.

"I wanna feel you too." He replied and then he got off me and stood up to his feet.

I watched him as he took off all of his clothes and began to size him up. He was perfect. The right height, measurements, skin color, the whole nine. And I couldn't keep my eyes off his big dick bulging from his boxer shorts. It was so fucking inviting.

At that very moment, I slid off my pants and my panties. I didn't have time to take off my shirt. I wanted his dick so badly. And he gave it to me.

He leaned into me and slowly pushed his manhood in me after he climbed back on top of me. I knew when he was entering inside of me that I needed for him to put on a condom but then I convinced myself that he had to be a man of integrity. He wouldn't fuck me in the raw if he had an STD. Would he? Once again, I was playing Russian Roulette with my life. This time it was in bed with a man I've only known for a few days. What was going on in my head?

The bad decision of fucking Julian in the raw faded away with every inch of dick he penetrated me with. My pussy was soaking wet. I spread my legs open so he could fuck every inch of my creamy pussy.

"Damn, this pussy feels so good," he complimented.

"Ahhh," I screamed out. "Oh God! Oh God! Oh God!" I hollered. My moans just drove him crazier. "C'mon . . . give it to me," I told him. I wrapped my legs up around his waist while he pounded me. "Owww!" I continued.

After several minutes with him on top, he got up and sat back down on the sofa in a seating position and pulled me on top of him. He wanted me to ride him. So I bounced up and down on that dick so hard and fast he was breathing like he had just run laps. "Oh, fuck me! Fuck me good," I talked much shit while I rode that dick.

"Oh shit, girl, your pussy is out of this fucking world," Julian growled. Just when I thought he was going to cum, I jumped up off his dick. "Wait...where you goin'?" he said, looking as if he was about to beg me to get back on it.

I laughed.

Then I turned around and got back on his dick backwards so he could see my whole ass, *the reverse cowgirl*. No man worth his salt could turn this shit down. Seeing a woman in this position made men's dicks harder and added to the throbbing sensation.

I bent over at the waist and pumped up and down on his dick again. "Awww fuck!" he moaned. He slapped my ass cheeks as I fucked the shit out of him. I planted my feet for leverage and then I used both of my hands and spread my ass cheeks apart so he could see his dick go in and out of my pussy. "I see it! Fuck me! I see it!" He called out. This was what us women live for—to drive a muthafucka crazy tapping that ass. It's called pussy whipping.

I started to feel myself about to cum because the shaft of his dick was pressing on my g-spot. "I'm coming!" I called out and then I sat up, closed my legs together and squeezed his dick with my pussy.

"Agggghhhh!" Julian bucked and screamed. He was coming as well. I jumped up quickly but I think some of his cum had got inside of me. I turned around and he started jerking the rest of his cum onto my tits. He started rubbing his dick and I watched it start to grow hard again.

"C'mere . . . we ain't finished yet," he said. Pulling me back down onto him, he and I went for rounds two, three and even, four. We finally ended up in my bed where I collapsed from exhaustion. He kept telling me repeatedly how beautiful I was. He even complimented me about how he loved my positive energy. That really threw me for a loop. No one has ever told me that I had positive energy. So, what was his deal? And what was this guy really trying to say?

Our Rendezvous

I thought after I rendezvous ended, Mr. Julian would put on his clothes and call it a night. To my surprise, he wanted to lie next to me and snuggle. I thought it was the most romantic thing ever. I think I'm falling for this guy. We lied there until we both fell asleep.

Unfortunately for me, my sleep was interrupted by the constant ringing of his freaking cell phone. When I looked at the clock on my DVR player, I noticed that it was 4 o'clock in the morning. I turned over and looked at him while he answered the call. "Twenty-four Hour Bail Services," I heard him say.

I couldn't hear what the caller was saying, but it didn't take a rocket scientist to know that it was a person calling for his professional services this time of the morning. The fact that my sleep was interrupted was what I had a problem with.

I finally laid my head back down after Julian got out of my bed to get dressed. "I've gotta meet this guy's girlfriend down at the jail so I can help her get him out. It sounds like he got jammed up by selling dope to an undercover cop." He explained.

"I understand. Take care of your business." I murmured.

"Can I see you later?" he asked me.

"Just call me and we'll see." I replied. I actually loved the idea of seeing him later. I just didn't want him to know it.

Without saying another word, he walked around the bed, leaned over and kissed me on the forehead. The kiss was so soft and gentle. I was about to melt. It was just the little things he did that got me warm and fuzzy.

Immediately after he kissed me, I watched him walk out of my bedroom. "Come lock your door," he yelled from the living room.

"I'm getting up now," I told him as I dragged myself out of bed. After I locked the door I watched him walk to his car from my living room window. The way he walked was so attractive. He had swag out of this world.

I walked away from the window after I saw him drive away and thought to myself that maybe he and I could become an item. Was love finally knocking on my doorstep?

I didn't get much sleep after Julian left. I tossed and turned all fucking night. So, I got up around 7 a.m. and toyed with the idea of being in a serious relationship with Julian. He seemed like the perfect guy. Handsome with a nice build. Very compassionate. Thoughtful and considerate. His dick was good as hell and he seemed like a woman pleaser. I need that type of man in my life. I just hoped that I won't screw it up with my obsessiveness of having all of my ex-husband's mistresses killed. I swear I want to let down my guard to love another man. But will it ever happen?

A few hours passed by while I lied back on my living room and watched TV. One minute I was thinking about Julian and then I'd start thinking about whether or not my hit man killed the next bitch on my list. I swear I hated those bitches. Just thinking about them gave me a bad taste in my mouth. They fucked up my marriage so they got to pay for it.

While I thought about the demise of my ex-husband's mistresses, my cell phone rang. I looked down at the caller ID and saw that it was Mrs. Elaine was calling me, so I answered the phone after the first ring. "Hello," I said.

"Good morning Kim," she greeted me.

"Hi Mrs. Elaine, how is everything?" I asked her.

"Well, I just got off the phone with Tammy and she just told me that William woke up out of his coma a few minutes ago. He was able to say a few words to her but the doctor says that he's still in critical condition and requires a breathing mask."

"And this happened a few minutes ago?" I asked, somewhat shocked at the fact that this motherfucker was conscious. My whole plan to have this bastard killed has gone out the fucking window.

"Yes. And the girls are so happy. I plan to take them up to the hospital to see him in a couple of hours because Tammy said the detectives will likely come and speak to him very soon so they can get his account about what happened. And since she doesn't want the girls to hear any of the ghastly details, I was wondering if you'd like to meet us up there later?"

"I've kind of got a lot of things I've got to do today. But as soon as I'm done, I can call you and see if you're still there. And if you are, I could probably stop by then." I lied. I wasn't trying to be anywhere around that motherfucker while he's alive and breathing. I want his ass dead!

"Okay, fair enough. So, call me later and I guess we'll go from there." Mrs. Elaine said.

"Sounds great! Send William my best!" I commented.

"I most certainly will." She agreed and then we disconnected our call.

I didn't hesitate to get my hit man on the phone because we needed to come up with a plan B. Or else my life as I know it was going to be fucked!